CW00321917

compact companions

PHILIPS *Classics*

COMPACT COMPANIONS

HANDEL

in association with CLASSIC *f*M

STEPHEN PETTITT

BCA

LONDON   NEW YORK   SYDNEY   TORONTO

To my mother, and in memory of William Day

First published in Great Britain in 1994 by

PAVILION BOOKS LIMITED

26 UPPER GROUND

LONDON SE1 9PD

Designed by Wherefore Art? Edited by Emma Lawson

Printed and bound in Singapore by Imago Publishing Ltd.

2 4 6 8 10 9 7 5 3

This edition published 1994 by BCA

by arrangement with PAVILION BOOKS LTD

CN 1376

CONTENTS

Handel in a painting by William Hogarth

Introduction

THE ESSENCE OF HANDEL

E ven if not by habit a listener to serious music, anyone would probably be able to recognize some Handel. The *Hallelujah Chorus* from *Messiah*, for instance, surely comes as close as it is possible to come to being a universally recognized piece, even though perhaps not everyone is aware of what work it comes in, or where, or why. Parts, at least, of the *Water Music* are widely known, if only from memories of organ voluntaries heard at family weddings. Some of his ceremonial music, like the Coronation Anthem *Zadok the Priest*, might also have a familiar ring. But where do these pieces fit in the history of music, or in the pattern of Handel's long life? And exactly what is it that makes his music so special?

Since the premise of this book assumes keenness rather than prior knowledge on the part of the reader, it is perhaps wisest to begin at the beginning and attempt to place Handel in his era. He is a composer of the high baroque period, which is to say that his working life occupied the first half of the eighteenth century, almost exactly coinciding with the working life of that other great German-born composer, Johann Sebastian Bach. Both inherited a rich and flourishing musical tradition. Earlier German composers of the seventeenth century, people like Heinrich Schütz, Johann Schein, Samuel Scheidt, and later on Dietrich Buxtehude, less well known than Handel or Bach but still important figures in their own right, had taken German music from the late renaissance, absorbed influences from Italy, mixed them with their own heritage, and so gave German music a strong identity. Nowhere was that identity stronger than in the sacred music which predominated in Germany at the time. The German form of the originally Italian sacred concerto, as cultivated by Schütz, prevailed in the south. In the north, the new form of the sacred cantata held sway. This form could be defined as a multi-movement sequence of choruses, arias and connecting narrative recitatives with a text derived from scriptural sources, often transformed into a form acceptable for the music by a distinguished poet, all with instrumental accompaniment. Bach wrote 200 or so sacred cantatas, and Handel himself cultivated the sacred cantata form, but only in his teenage years when he worked as an organist in Halle. Unfortunately, no German sacred cantata by him survives. But the many secular cantatas he wrote a little later in Italy do.

Agostino Steffani: composer, diplomat and priest

Since Monteverdi's *Orfeo*, composed in 1607, opera had been popular in Italy. By the time of Handel's youth it had also begun to flourish in major German centres like Hamburg. It was sung with no deference to the language of the country in which it was being performed. Indeed, it was Italians who were often responsible for performances. Agostino Steffani, for instance, directed the opera in Hanover. It was not long before the young Handel found himself working in Hamburg, so almost from the very beginning his musical environment was one in which two different streams tugged at each other. But where Bach, though by no means uninfluenced by Italian music, preferred to stay in his home country, gaining local success with his sacred and chamber music, Handel was lured to Italy in 1706 to find out what the fuss was all about. Once in Rome he quickly established himself there and enjoyed considerable success. He was able to mix with the cream of Italian musicians in the luxuriant palaces of the moneyed and cultured cardinals. Not unnaturally, being young and impressionable, he absorbed into his style a number of Italianate characteristics: a general openness and

Georg Ludwig, Elector of Hanover and King of England

flexibility of manner, a distinctive, direct tunefulness, and a penchant for elegant decoration. He also got to grips with the latest and most fashionable forms, learning much, as his own instrumental concertos and sonatas reveal, from the elegance and economy of Corelli.

In November 1710 he visited England for the first time. The liberal terms of his employment with the Elector of Hanover, Georg Ludwig, to whom he had been appointed Kapellmeister (Master of the Chapel) in June of that year, and who in 1714 was to succeed to the English throne as George I, helped him strengthen his links with London, although until that succession occurred there was occasionally conflict between his courtly duties and his free spirit. Once permanently installed in London in 1712, commissions from two important patrons, the Duke of Marlborough and James Brydges (shortly to become Duke of Chandos), occupied much of his time. But his taste for composing operas had begun early and had blossomed in Italy with the successful staging of *Agrippina* in Venice in 1710. He had prepared the ground for that success much earlier. *Almira*, his first opera, had been seen in Hamburg in 1705. He was the right man for the Royal Academy of Music, a society of patrons intent on bringing Italian opera to the London stage, to choose as its first 'Master of the Orchestra with a Sallary'.

England was to prove him a bold entrepreneur as well as a great composer. But after enduring the rivalries of the Opera of the Nobility from 1733 and the attempts of others to forge a successful English operatic style with the staging of John Gay's *The Beggar's Opera* in 1728, Handel's brand of opera ultimately failed to win the enduring sympathy of the public, despite his many attempts at adapting the genre to suit the particular moods and tastes of the times. So, under economic as well as artistic and social pressures, he eventually employed another tactic: the adaptation of the Italian oratorio, at which he had excelled early in his career, to suit English conditions. In truth, the adaptation was so radical that the two varieties, English and Italian, bear the scantest relationship with each other. The English oratorio involved subjects of high moral import and used choruses extensively. It was geared to appeal to a broad middle-class public, where Handel's Italian oratorios had been designed for the pleasure of the ecclesiastical nobility. The new form was cheap to stage since on the whole it was not staged at all. Importantly, the words could be understood, and the music was concise but colourfully expressive and often intentionally impressive too, though it is easy to read too much grandiosity into what Handel wrote.

Handel was never conscious of writing for posterity. When he sat down to compose, it was usually for the express purpose of filling a theatre. He did revive works, but he worked in an era when there was always a demand for something new. If something succeeded and made him money, all well and good. If not, the next work might. In our own age, when composers gifted or indifferent gaze into the infinite and consciously try to produce profound and enduring statements about the human condition and the universe, such an attitude might seem strange. But we can perhaps liken Handel's approach to that of a composer like Andrew Lloyd Webber today. His job was to write a show, stage it, take the money if any came in, invest it in the next show. If the music was good it might endure. But that, for Handel, was a bonus.

The essence of Handel's music is not grandeur, as those unaware of the real extent of his output might assume, but theatre. So beware: works like the *Coronation Anthems*, the *Music for the Royal Fireworks*, the *Water Music* and so on, though immensely popular both in their own time and today, are in a sense untypical, even though they do the jobs for which they were intended with real inspiration, never mere efficiency.

A NOTE ON HANDEL'S BORROWINGS

Assessments of Handel's standing have often been unnecessarily complicated by the common knowledge of his practice of taking other composers' ideas and reworking them in his own music. Some have adopted resolutely moralistic stances on this matter, claiming in effect that he was too lazy to think of ideas of his own. They apply the same censorious attitude to his self-borrowings. Those tempted to wring their hands in horror at this practice should, however, bear in mind one fact: that what a composer does with his ideas is more indicative of his gifts than those ideas themselves. Context and the realization of possibilities are everything.

A Cosmopolitan's Life and Works

GERMANY 1685–1706

George Frederick Handel, as his name now tends to be spelt in English-speaking countries, was born with the name Georg Friederich Händel in Halle, Germany, on 23 February, 1685. It was the year that saw the birth of two other great baroque composers, Johann Sebastian Bach and Domenico Scarlatti; Handel's father, also called Georg, was a barber-surgeon of some repute; he was well into his sixties when Handel was born. His mother, Dorothea Taust, was the daughter of a local pastor.

The entry of Handel's birth in the record of baptisms in Liebrauenkirche, Halle

Comparatively little is known of Handel's earliest years. Much of the information we have comes from the *Memoirs of the Life of the Late George Frederic Handel* – written anonymously – by John Mainwaring, a cleric and Lady Margaret Professor in Divinity at St John's College, Cambridge. This book, published in the 1760s, was conceived through a process akin to Chinese whispers. Mainwaring obtained his information from John Christopher Smith the younger, who was the son of Handel's copyist of the same name. He was a minor composer in his own right, and gave considerable help to Handel in the latter's old age, when he became blind. But much of the information in this book has been proved to be incorrectly dated. Another early source of information

The birthplace of Handel in Halle, Saxony

is the volume of *Anecdotes of George Frederick Handel and John Christopher Smith*, collected, again anonymously, by Smith's stepson William Coxe and published in 1799.

Like many great composers, Handel proved himself innately musical at an early age, but his father refused to allow his talents to flourish and apparently attempted to prevent him from gaining access to any musical instruments. He was set on a sturdy career in law for his son. But stifled talent has a habit of asserting itself with all the more determination, and the story goes that Handel practised in secret on a clavichord, the quietest of keyboard instruments, which somehow he managed to smuggle into the attic of the family home. One fine day, this probably apocryphal tale continues, the Handel family visited the court of Saxe-Weissenfels, where Handel's father was court surgeon and his older half-brother, Karl, a servant. Handel got to play the organ, duly impressing the duke, who urged his father to allow the son to study music and law simultaneously. Whether or not this story is true, what happened next is beyond dispute. Handel took lessons from Friedrich Wilhelm Zachow, who was a prolific and highly respected composer and the organist at the Liebfrauenkirche (or Marienkirche) in Halle. Zachow instructed Handel in imitating different styles as well as in playing violin, organ and harpsichord.

Handel playing the clavier in the attic,
Woldemar Friedrich's impression of Handel's youth, 1878

Apparently he was also required to compose a number of original cantatas for performance in the church, though none is known to have survived.

Mainwaring suggests that Handel and his father then visited the court of the Electress Sophia Charlotte of Brandenburg in Berlin, where he met the Italian composers Giovanni Bononcini and Attilio Ariosti. He was invited to enter the Elector's service and asked to go to Italy for further tutelage. The story goes that, because of his father's infirmity, he refused both the invitation and the request, but

Mainwaring's chronology is suspect. In fact, Ariosti did not get to Berlin, and so could not have met Handel, until after the death of Handel's father.

Handel matriculated at the University of Halle on 10 February 1702. On 13 March he was appointed organist at the Calvinist Cathedral, replacing the disreputable – and sacked – Johann Christoph Leporin for a probationary year in exchange for free lodging and a modest salary of fifty thalers. Among his duties were 'to prelude on the prescribed Psalms and Spiritual Songs', which presumably meant improvising.

Among the friends Handel cultivated at Halle was the composer Georg Philipp Telemann, born in 1681, who had been sent to study at Leipzig, some twenty miles from Halle. The two corresponded and visited each other frequently, exchanging ideas, and their friendship was to be a lifelong one. Telemann introduced Handel to opera; and it was very likely this revelation which persuaded Handel to leave provincial Halle in 1703 for the cosmopolitan allure of Hamburg. The opera house there was under the control of Reinhard Keiser, a dissolute man but an important composer of operas. Handel was appointed as a rank-and-file second violinist at the opera, and later played the harpsichord for the orchestra. Under Keiser's patronage, Handel's first operas, *Almira* and *Nero* (the latter now lost), received their first performances in Hamburg in 1705. (Keiser's awareness of a potentially threatening

Georg Philipp Telemann, composer and friend, in an engraving of 1744

Prospect and ground view of Hamburg
in an engraving of 1690
by Johann Baptista Homann

rival may or may not have been the spur for his decision to compose operas on the same subjects soon afterwards.)

Keiser was the most distinguished composer of opera at this time. In Hamburg he had a large orchestra at his service and so could afford extravagant musical effects. This invaluable resource was used with relish by Handel in *Almira*. Keiser's music was also the source for many of the ideas which Handel used in his work, something noted as early as 1745 by Johann Scheibe in his *Critischer Musikus*, where he writes that Handel showed 'great understanding and powerful deliberation' when dealing with Keiser's original material – that is, he explored and developed it and put it into its appropriate context. That became understood when Chrysander's Complete Handel Edition project published Keiser's opera *Octavia* in 1902 as a supplement to the main series. In *Octavia* can be found the source, for instance, of the aria from *Messiah*, 'Comfort ye my people'. Handel kept copies of many other of Keiser's operas, and used them just as flagrantly for many of his other good ideas. It has become something of a musicologist's game to spot these things, as it has to discover Handel's quarrying and reworking of his own material. What is important, however, is how Handel uses his models, transforming them to suit his own purpose.

Once in Hamburg, Handel, already demonstrating a gregarious personality, quickly made the acquaintance of Johann Mattheson, a composer who also acted, sang, wrote and played the harpsichord. Mattheson's accounts *Grundlage einer Ehren-Pforte*, a collection of biographies (including Handel's) published without Handel's cooperation in 1740, and *Georg Friedrich Händels Lebensbeschreibung* (1761), provide more valuable though not totally reliable source material for Handel's biography. This artistic polymath seems rather pompously to have assumed responsibility for taking Handel in hand and teaching him a thing or two, despite being only four years his senior. Indeed, he claims to have led him scene by scene through the composition of *Almira* and to have taught him how to write good melodies by exposing him to the musical scene of Hamburg. In August 1703, Mattheson and Handel travelled together to Lübeck, visiting the composer Buxtehude with a view to succession in the post of organist there. But since one condition of the appointment was that the holder should marry Buxtehude's daughter, and since she apparently appealed to the tastes of neither of them (nor to that of J.S. Bach, who made a famously arduous visit for the same professional purpose two years later), they turned down the offer.

Handel was subsequently introduced by Mattheson to the English Resident, or

Ambassador, in Hamburg, John Wyche, who engaged him as harpsichord teacher to his son Cyril. Not only did this give Handel some welcome financial respite; for perhaps the first time, he began to consider life beyond Germany. Soon, however, Mattheson replaced Handel in this job, suggesting perhaps a touch of envy by the older man for the younger. There was further trouble between the two at the end of 1704. Mattheson explains his version of the incident in his 1740 publication.

> *On 5 December . . . when my third opera,* Cleopatra, *was being performed with Handel at the harpsichord, a misunderstanding arose . . . I as composer directed and at the same time sang the part of Antonius, who about half an hour before the end commmits suicide. Until this occasion I had been accustomed after this action to go into the orchestra and accompany the rest myself, which unquestionably the author can do better than anyone else. But this time Handel refused to give up his place. Incited by onlookers we fought a duel at the door of the Opera House, in the open market place and in front of a crowd of onlookers.*

Mattheson goes on to explain that his sword was broken, and Handel saved by his coat button, but that the two were quickly reconciled and by 30 December were dining together again, apparently better friends than before. Mainwaring's version is slightly different. According to him, Mattheson attacked without due warning and Handel's life was saved only by the score of *Cleopatra* he had coincidentally pressed against his chest.

Already, Handel was composing at a great rate, although no autographs survive from the Hamburg period. Mainwaring claims that he 'made a considerable number of Sonatas'; while a large quantity of keyboard music, including suites and partitas and his two largest sets of chaconne-variations, has been presumed to belong to the period.

*The German composer
Dietrich Buxtehude
in an allegory
of friendship with
the organist
and composer
Johann Adam Reincken*

Other compositions from this time have been discredited. For instance, a *St John Passion*, first performed on Good Friday 1704, is now considered to be the work of Keiser, Handel's boss at the opera.

Almira, however, was most definitely by Handel. It received its première at the Hamburg opera on 8 January 1705 and ran for twenty nights, with Mattheson singing the title role. Handel followed it up swiftly with the now lost work that went by the long-winded title, *Die durch Blut und Mord erlangete Liebe, oder: Nero*, with the same librettist as for *Almira*, Friedrich Christian Feustking. But *Nero's* run lasted for just three performances and dissatisfaction was expressed, by others and ultimately by Handel himself, for both of Feustking's librettos. For his next two operas, *Florindo* and

The young composer in a portrait by Sir James Thornhill

Daphne (again, both now lost), Handel used a different librettist, Hinrich Hinsch. In the meantime, Keiser had relinquished the lease of the Hamburg opera in 1707, and by the time the two new operas came to be performed in Hamburg in January 1708, Handel had already settled in the pleasanter climate of Rome, a hotbed of music-making. He had already witnessed enough of the trials and tribulations, as well as the triumphs, of running an opera house to be able to use the experience to his own immense advantage later.

ITALY, 1706–1710

E xactly who or what lured Handel to Italy we are not sure. Mainwaring tells of an encounter between Handel and the Prince Ferdinand de' Medici of Florence in Hamburg, at which the Prince prevailed upon Handel to make the journey. Handel, though disparaging about the fruits of Italian culture, was convinced to go, but resolved to do so 'on his own bottom', to quote Mainwaring, rather than take the Prince's offer of a trip with all expenses paid. Mattheson, on the other hand, says that Handel went to Italy for free with Herr von Binitz, apparently a friend and benefactor. Mainwaring details Handel's travels through Italy with somewhat confused chronology. But there is no reason to doubt the truth of at least the basics of his principle claim, since the anecdote must have come from the horse's mouth. Whatever, it is now possible, thanks to recent research into the archives of the Ruspoli family (Handel's chief patron in Rome was the Marchese Francesco Ruspoli) to reconstruct in some detail the sequence of events that led from *Almira* and *Nero* in Hamburg to the première of *Agrippina* in Venice in 1709–10, though there are still gaps to be filled.

FLORENCE, ROME, NAPLES

In all likelihood, and just as Mainwaring says, Handel first went to Florence on Ferdinand de' Medici's invitation in the autumn of 1706. His opera *Rodrigo* was staged at the Accademia degli Infuocati there around October 1707, so he could well have been there involving himself in negotiations for that event. By January 1707 he had reached Rome, as an entry in Valesio's diary tells us. 'A Sassone has arrived . . . who is an excellent harpsichordist and composer. Today he showed his prowess by playing the organ at the church of St John to the admiration of all.' Handel seems to have made his mark on the city with amazing rapidity. Besides ingratiating himself to Pamphili, Handel made the acquaintance of three influential cardinals, Benedetto Ruspoli, the

Above: A panorama of Rome listing the eighty churches which dominate the city, 1740
Below: Kaspar van Wittel's painting of Rome looking up the Tiber to St Peter's and the Vatican

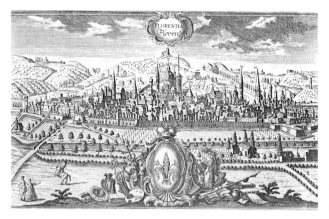

*A copperplate engraving
of Florence, 1740,
by Johann Georg Ringlin*

indulgent Pietro Ottoboni, and Carlo Colonna. Ottoboni employed the famous violinist-composer Arcangelo Corelli as the leader of his orchestra, and held a concert every Wednesday under Corelli's direction. Handel's writing for the violin at this time was deeply influenced by Corelli's technical skills, though it shows more fire than the Italian's rather refined music for his own instrument. Mainwaring tells us of the famous competition between Handel and Domenico Scarlatti, which was staged at Ottoboni's own behest in his palace. We do not know who the adjudicators were, but this good-natured duel between the two best keyboard players in Europe – Handel achieved that reputation early – ended indecisively as far as the harpsichord playing was concerned. When it came to the part of the competition held on the organ, however, Scarlatti himself readily conceded that Handel was the superior artist. Mainwaring points out the different manner of each player's performance. Scarlatti, he says, showed 'certain elegance and delicacy of expression', whereas Handel possessed 'an uncommon brilliance and command of finger' with 'an amazing fulness, force, and energy'. So in his playing, so in his compositions, he adds.

Before May 1707 Handel had composed his first oratorio, *Il trionfo del Tempo e del Disinganno*. The text was provided by Pamphili, at whose palace the first performance may also have taken place. This work was to prove enduring. Handel made two more versions of it at different stages later in his life.

But why oratorio, which was not fully staged with action, instead of opera? Simply because a papal prohibition had been put in place in 1697. Opera was not allowed in public performance in Rome, so composers went for what they saw as the next best thing. Oratorios and cantatas were subjected to the most lavish productions, operatic to a large degree,

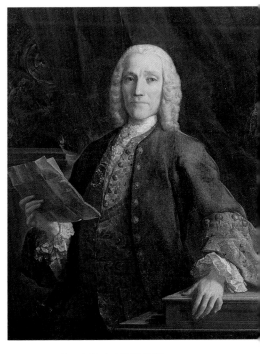

Domenico Scarlatti (1685–1757)

with the very best singers and players engaged to perform it. Even so, in *Il Trionfo*, Handel stumbled across an unexpected hazard. Corelli, that most illustrious violinist, had difficulty in playing the work's Overture. Mainwaring recounts Corelli's words: 'Ma, caro Sassone (said he) questa Musica è nel stylo Francese, di ch'io non m'intendo' [But, dear Saxon, this music is in the French style, which I don't understand]. A footnote remarks that Handel bowed to circumstance and substituted something in the less fiery Italian style. Also dating from this time are the psalm-motets now thought to be part of a project to set the Vespers service for the Feast of Our Lady of Mount Carmel. These pieces include the well-known *Dixit Dominus*.

Handel himself was not primarily employed by Ottoboni. He enjoyed to a greater degree the patronage of the Marchese Francesco Ruspoli. He was appointed as a household musician to Ruspoli for at least three separate periods, from May to October 1707, from February to May 1708, and from July to November 1708. It was a freelance contract, without salary but with the expectation that he would compose regularly. His colleagues included Margherita Durastante, the renowned soprano who later followed Handel to London, as well as the distinguished violinists Domenico and Pietro Castrucci. Handel wrote copiously for Ruspoli. The list includes the oratorio *La Resurrezione*, three Latin motets, eight cantatas with high instruments, two hybrid cantatas with Spanish and French texts (*No se emederà jamàs* and *Sans y penser*, the former with guitar accompaniment), and at least forty cantatas for solo voice and continuo. Almost all of the cantatas were written for Durastante to sing; they would be performed at Ruspoli's so-called *conversazione* each Sunday afternoon.

In the autumn of 1707 Handel returned briefly to Florence for the opening performances of the first of his Italian operas, *Rodrigo*, at the public theatre in the via del Cocomero. For his troubles, Handel received 100 sequins and a dinner service.

Much of the music was later recycled in various works by the composer, who seems not to have been particularly pleased either with the libretto or his own response to it, even though the production was actually a great success. The opera could well have yielded other, more sensual benefits. His leading lady, Vittoria Tarquini, a favourite of Ferdinand de' Medici, according to Mainwaring transferred her affections from nobleman to composer. Doubt has been cast on this tale by the absence of Tarquini's name on the word-book, but a letter written by Electress Sophia of Hanover in 1710 again refers to widespread gossip that Handel was Tarquini's lover.

By early 1708 he seems to have been back in Rome with Ruspoli. His next major task was to compose *La Resurrezione*. This was Handel's first exercise at a sacred work in this genre. Ruspoli presented the work lavishly and expensively in the great hall of his palace on Easter Day that year. Handel was given plenty of time to write and revise the piece, and for once there was adequate rehearsal and a guaranteed repeat performance on Easter Monday. Durastante headed the soloists. Ruspoli hoped to impress Pope Clement XI with the lavish staging, and even arranged for music stands to be specially built and decorated with his and his wife's coats of arms. The decor involved representations of the characters, the work's title spectacularly backlit, cherubs, a picture of the resurrection, and much velvet and gold, taffeta and rosettes. Valesio's diary briefly records the work's success, but the Pope quickly took Ruspoli to task for allowing a female singer to take part. A male substitute, a castrato known only as 'Filippo', sang in Durastante's place in the second performance.

Before the end of April, Handel set off on his travels once more. His destination was Naples, where, at the Duke of Alvito's house, he produced a cantata and the serenata *Aci, Galatea e Polifemo*. Opera was quite legal in Naples and indeed flourished there. But the serenata was commissioned for performance at a wedding, for which a fully

Naples: with the Castel del'Ovo, Palazzo Reale and Certosa di San Martino in view in a painting by Gaspar van Wittel

fledged opera would hardly be appropriate. Mainwaring stirs rumours of another romantic liaison, with one Donna Laura who is supposed to have commissioned the piece, but no evidence exists to confirm this or otherwise. (Incidentally, the story of *Aci, Galatea e Polifemo* is exactly the same as that of *Acis and Galatea*, which Handel wrote a few years later at Cannons Park, though the music is entirely different.)

Aci, Galatea e Polifemo was a pastoral work, and its composition proved that Handel had by now become very much at ease within the orbit of the so-called Accademia degli Arcadi. This was an alliance of noblemen and artists that had come together in the closing years of the seventeenth century with the avowed purpose of restoring to Italian art – and specifically its poetry – its directness and naturalness, which were in danger of becoming subsumed by mannerism. Each member of the group was assigned a pastoral pseudonym. Corelli, for example, was Arcimelo; Alessandro Scarlatti became Terpando. The group held meetings in what they called cabins and woods, though in fact they were palaces and grounds. The host changed from year to year. In July 1708 it was Ruspoli's turn, so naturally many of Handel's cantatas composed around this time were written to Arcadian texts.

Florence, Venice, Innsbruck, Hanover, Halle, Düsseldorf

I mmediately after the autumn of 1708 we know little of Handel's movements and projects. But by March 1709 he was back with Ferdinand de' Medici in Florence. In November 1709 he left that city, bound for Innsbruck with a letter of recommendation from Ferdinand addressed to Prince Carl von Neuberg. His first major stop, however, was Venice. In Venice, operas flourished as nowhere else, though the English visitor Joseph Addison, in his *Remarks on Several Parts of*

The piazza of San Marco, Venice

Copperplate engraving of Venice, 1740

Italy &c, published in 1705, had earlier robustly criticized the words and plots which they usually involved. Handel's *Agrippina*, composed to a libretto by Cardinal Vincenzo Grimani, was staged in the Cardinal's family's theatre, the Teatro di San Giovanni Crisostomo. The work opened just after Christmas 1709 and enjoyed a record run that extended well into the New Year. What his audiences probably did not know was that Handel composed only five completely new arias for the work. The rest had come from his own earlier music and from pieces by Keiser and Mattheson, judiciously chosen and reworked.

Among the audiences at performances of *Agrippina* were two foreign representatives: Baron Kielmansegge, Master of the Horse to the Elector of Hanover, and Charles Montagu, Earl of Manchester and British Ambassador. Both, though well aware that Handel was on his way to Innsbruck, attempted to headhunt him, the German egged on by Prince Ernst of Hanover (the Elector's brother), the Briton encouraged by Joseph Smith, a resident of Venice, patron of Canaletto and a banker of renown. Handel, however, went to Innsbruck (we do not know exactly when), but had already left by early March, 1710.

His first stop was Hanover, where he was greeted warmly by the composer-turned-diplomat-turned-cleric, Agostino Steffani. Mainwaring recounts that Kielmansegge introduced Handel to the Elector, who offered him 1,500 crowns to stay in the city. But Handel apparently protested that he had commitments to fulfil elsewhere and so managed to secure an agreement whereby he was free to be absent immediately for a year or even more, and to go wherever he liked. Under such conditions, on 16 June 1710 he became Hanover's Kapellmeister and left shortly afterwards for Halle, where

Düsseldorf in an engraving by Martin Engelbrecht

A copperplate engraving
of Hanover by F. B. Werner

he saw his ailing mother and his old teacher Zachow, and for Düsseldorf. In Düsseldorf, the Elector Palatine's pleasure in seeing him and the impact of his brilliant exhibitions on the harpsichord were tempered by disappointment that he had already committed himself elsewhere.

ENGLAND 1710

C ommitments he may have had, but Handel's sights were set on further journeying. Instead of going back to his new employer, he continued to travel. At the end of 1710, in the unencouraging month of November, he set foot for the first time on English soil. It could not have been the happiest introduction. Not only was there the greyness, damp and cold, but London, then as now, was dirty and polluted. The contrast with Italy cannot have been more marked. What is remarkable is Handel's keenness at least to sound out the place. As far as we know, there was no contract to allure him.

Music-drama in London at the beginning of the century was essentially a mixture of music and words, the Purcellian 'semi-opera', which itself had been spawned from the court masque. Even Purcell's one true opera, *Dido and Aeneas*, was revived within the

England: Canaletto's panorama of the Thames from the terrace of Somerset House

framework of spoken drama in the first decade of the century. Efforts had been made to import Italian opera in the first few years of the century, but with little success, owing to the employment of second-rate Italian singers and botched adaptations. But in March 1706 Bononcini's *Camilla*, adapted by Nicola Haym, the Italian cellist, composer, librettist and antiquarian, who at this time was chamber musician to the second Duke of Bedford, was seen at the Drury Lane Theatre, and the tide began to turn. *Camilla* was widely admired, setting off a train of events that, significantly, included the importation of Italian singers. In particular, there were the famed castrati, singers

who as boys were blessed with particularly fine voices, the elements of which were preserved in adulthood by the brutal but widespread practice of castration. Italian opera, rather than an English variety which began to be cultivated by composers such as Johann Christoph Pepusch and John Eccles towards the end of the first decade of the century, became fashionable in London.

When Handel arrived in London his music was not entirely unknown. Parts of *Rodrigo* had been used as incidental music in Ben Johnson's *The Alchemist* and published by John Walsh the elder, though not under Handel's name, in 1710. Arias from *Agrippina* were brought to London and shamelessly placed in other operatic contexts. But it took Handel almost no time at all to establish a real success. Aaron Hill, manager of the Queen's Theatre

The German-born composer Johann Christoph Pepusch who settled in London in 1704

in the Haymarket, provided an outline, and the theatre's own librettist, Giacomo Rossi, the actual words, for *Rinaldo*, which Handel put together in a matter of a fortnight, thanks again to numerous borrowings. Nicolini, the most celebrated castrato yet imported from Italy, was the star, and for him at least Handel wrote new music. Joseph Addison and Sir Richard Steele, in *The Spectator*, savaged the sets and the scene-changing, but the opera nevertheless took London by storm and ran for fifteen nights. Walsh duly published the arias and instrumental music under Handel's own name, and Handel was introduced at Court.

At this time he also met a little girl, Mary Granville, who subsequently, as Mrs Pendarves and Mrs Delany, became a lifelong friend. Her autobiography and correspondence (published in London 1861–2) includes many invaluable references to the composer's day-to-day affairs and to the peaks and troughs of his career in London.

HANOVER AND BACK TO LONDON

O nce the London season had finished, Handel dutifully returned to Hanover via Düsseldorf, and his life became somewhat calmer. Mainwaring mentions a few unspecified compositions, but there was no great operatic work to occupy him. He inevitably became restless, and in the autumn of 1712 asked his employer once again for permission to take leave of absence in order to visit England. The Elector, according to Mainwaring, agreed on condition that Handel returned within a 'reasonable' time. Back in London, he found a supporter, one Mr Andrews of Barn-Elms (Barnes), and in

November 1712 his *Il pastor fido* was first seen at the Queen's Theatre. *Rinaldo*'s success was not repeated. The piece was conceived with all the limitations of the Italian 'Arcadian' pieces, and was performed without star singers, which suited the public not one jot. The composer reacted with typical swiftness to his own failure. In December he finished the highly dramatic, five-act opera *Teseo*, whose successful staging, again at the Queen's Theatre, in January 1713 was marred only by the theatre manager Owen Swiney's disappearance with two nights' takings. The then assistant manager of the Haymarket Theatre, the Swiss émigré John Jacob Heidegger, stepped into the breach, and the singers formed a cooperative.

BURLINGTON HOUSE AND GEORGE I'S ACCESSION

*T*eseo's libretto, by Nicolas Haym, was dedicated to Lord Burlington, who subsequently became Handel's patron and offered him accommodation in Burlington House, Piccadilly. He stayed there for three years, largely left to his own devices but able to associate freely with the most eminent artists and intellectuals in the land. He naturally also took part in concert-giving. Sir John Hawkins's *A General History of the Science and Practice of Music* records Handel's visits to St Paul's Cathedral, then a brand new building, around this time to play the organ after service. Afterwards, he would adjourn to the Queen's Arms tavern for informal music and refreshment. The composer was well aware of the advisability of showing loyalty towards his host nation. Without apparently being commissioned, for the Thanksgiving Service on 14 January

1714 for Marlborough's Wars, which had ended with the Treaty of Utrecht, he composed a *Te Deum and Jubilate* in English. At about the same time he wrote the *Ode for the Birthday of Queen Anne*. The result of this slightly sycophantic industry was a handsome £200 per year pension from the monarch for life, perhaps a ploy intended to prise him away from his Hanoverian obligations.

If so, there was no resentment when, in September 1714, the Elector came to England, following Queen Anne's death, as George I. At a morning service which the new king attended, a *Te Deum* by Handel was sung. The story of the disgraced Handel ingratiating himself to a resentful George I by composing the *Water Music*, perpetrated by Mainwaring, has been more or less discredited.

A view of north London from across the Thames

*George I in a posthumous portrait
by Jacob-Christophe Le Blon, 1730*

Rinaldo was revived at what was now the King's Theatre in January 1715, with Nicolini again in the title role. The managers specifically asked for no demands for encores, for fear of lengthening the work too much. The next opera was *Amadigi,* whose libretto, by Heidegger, is dedicated to Burlington. The production must have involved some complex staging. An announcement in the *Daily Courant* on 25 May courteously asked that nobody, not even subscribers, should encroach upon the stage, a comment that gives some insight into the habits of contemporary audiences. But attendances were not quite as hoped for. Rival productions, including one of *Camilla*, indisposed singers, the threats of the Jacobites, all conspired against full houses. Nevertheless, things looked healthy enough for Handel. His finances were secure and, more importantly for us two-and-a-half centuries later, he was beginning to invest his drama with real characters and emotions.

Germany – the Recruiting of Schmidt –
Permanent Residence in England – Cannons

The following July, along with the King, Handel went back to Germany, where he probably visited his relatives in Halle and renewed his acquaintance with Johann Christoph Schmidt, an old fellow student who had made good in the wool trade in Ansbach. Schmidt was persuaded to return to London with Handel to become his assistant and treasurer. Once there, he anglicized his name to John Christopher Smith; his son, also John Christopher, was to become Handel's assistant from 1720. Perhaps it was during this visit that Handel composed the *Brockes Passion*, his last exercise in setting a German text, though Mattheson says that he wrote the work in England and subsequently posted it. The same text was also set by Keiser, Telemann and Mattheson. Was there some kind of competition between the four? J. S. Bach also copied Handel's setting for performance in Leipzig.

Handel returned to England in 1717, determined to stay for good. The King returned too, to find himself in the nation's bad books. Not suprisingly, for he was flaunting his extramarital affair with one Madame Schulenberg, was openly at odds with the Prince of Wales, and had refused to speak English. In an attempt to endear himself to his country he organized a concert on the River Thames. Friedrich Bonet, Prussian Ambassador at the time, writes of the occasion, describing the barge immediately behind that bearing the King's party as holding about fifty musicians who played music especially composed for the occasion by Handel. But conclusions should not be drawn too rapidly: Walsh did not publish *The Celebrated Water Musick*, as he called it, until 1733, and other evidence suggests that what we know as the

Water Music comes from several pieces composed for separate occasions.

The next major patron under whose protection Handel found himself was James Brydges, Earl of Carnarvon, who became Duke of Chandos in 1719 and who owned a palace, as yet unfinished, built in the Palladian style near Edgware, about ten miles north of London. Cannons was an extravagance not only as far as its building and grounds were concerned; the style of its day-to-day household activities was also lavish. The chapel employed instrumentalists and singers, and musicians played when the Duke was at table. Handel was engaged specifically as a composer, since there was already an established Director of Music, Johann Pepusch. The lifestyle he enjoyed was

An engraving of music being played to George I, with Handel in the king's boat, by Edouard Hamman

well away from the London limelight, which in any case would have been of little use, since the King's Theatre had reverted to masquerades in order to recoup losses incurred by Heidegger. There is little documentary information about Handel's life at this time, but a letter from Brydges to the polymath Dr John Arbuthnot mentions a number of anthems. The cycle of works in which these pieces were included was to become known collectively as the Chandos Anthems. These earliest examples were probably first performed in St Lawrence Church, Whitchurch, near Cannons, rather than in the household chapel, because building was still in progress. Other pieces dating from Handel's time at Cannons are *Acis and Galatea* and *Esther*, both pivotal works. Because Handel was involved in teaching the harpsichord and organ, a large quantity of keyboard music was also written in this period; it rapidly achieved wide circulation in manuscript copies. Handel quickly stepped in to get a collection of them published under the title *Suites de Pièces pour le clavecin*, so that he could cash in on its popularity.

OPERA IN EARNEST – THE ROYAL ACADEMY

Meanwhile, London was sorely missing its Italian opera, so in 1719, Mainwaring tells us, 'a project was formed by the Nobility for erecting an academy at the Haymarket . . . to secure themselves a constant supply of Operas to be composed by Handel, and performed under his direction.' The King allied himself to the project, which was called the Royal Academy. Heidegger was engaged as manager. The otherwise fairly flabby team of directors included the dramatist and architect Sir John

Vanbrugh. Handel was appointed 'master of the Orchestra with a Sallary'. By May, sixty-three subscribers had been enlisted, lured to subsidize the venture with the offer of two silver admission tickets valid for twenty-one years. (The money raised proved to be inadequate to sustain the Academy beyond 1728. In fact, there is no reason to believe that the promoters ever seriously had in mind an operation which would break even in the long term. Opera, then as now, was an expensive matter and always risked losing money.)

Handel was sent abroad to look for singers for the new company, and specifically to engage the services of the celebrated Italian castrato Senesino (whose real name was Francesco Bernardi) if he could. He journeyed to Dresden via Halle. In Dresden, an opera by the composer Antonio Lotti, *Teofane*, was in repertory, playing with a starry cast which happened to include Senesino, another castrato called Matteo Berselli, and two colleagues from Handel's time in Italy, Durastante and the bass Giuseppe Boschi. In the event, he managed only to engage Durastante for the Academy's first season, much to the derision of the Academy's official poet and librettist Paolo Rolli, who sneeringly called her an elephant.

Surviving papers of the Duke of Portland, who drew up the Academy's budgets, include lists of players, giving a valuable indication of typical size and composition of the opera pit band Handel had in mind at this time. The thirty-four instrumentalists on the books included eight first, five second and three third violins, together with four oboes, three bassoons and trumpet.

The Academy did not concentrate exclusively on Handel's operas, though his works naturally predominated. Bononcini and Ariosti were also represented. The Academy's first season opened on 2 April 1720 with a work by Giovanni Porta called *Numitore*. Handel's offering, *Radamisto*, was reserved for the King's first visit. It was a grand success. But difficulties lay ahead. That summer the South Sea Bubble, the speculative mania associated with the South Sea Company, which, in return for exclusive trading rights with Spanish America and the South Seas, had taken over the national debt, burst. The fortunes of many rich people, as well as their reputations, were lost. Even so, the Academy, after changes in the composition of its directorate, was able to open its second season on 19 November 1720, now with Senesino freshly arrived from Italy as its star attraction.

Bononcini's *Astarto* was the chief success of this season; a revision of Handel's *Radamisto*, which opened on 28 December 1720, ran for only seven performances. Later, the Academy came up with a hybrid work, *Muzio Scevola*, which was written by three different composers, presumably in order to save time. Act I was by the Opera's principal cellist Filippo Amadei, Act II by Bononcini, and Act III by Handel himself. The following season, *Radamisto* was staged again, and again substantially revised for the purpose. On 9 December, 1721 there was also the première of a new opera to a libretto by Rolli, *Floridante*, which the historian and diarist Charles Burney thought superior in every way to what Bononcini had to offer. But still Bononcini had the upper hand in terms of numbers of performances. The public liked to imagine the two composers battling it out for supremacy; closer to the truth was that each admired the other. They were, in any case, different kinds of composers, as was already widely recognized. Handel wrote dramatic, heroic, passionate music; Bononcini was more adept at the sort of Italianate pastoralism cultivated by the Roman Arcadians.

For the 1722–3 season a new singer, Francesca Cuzzoni, arrived from Italy. She made her debut on 12 January 1723 in Handel's *Ottone*, the opera which is the source of a lovely though possibly apocryphal story concerning Handel's ways with his prima donnas. According to Mainwaring, Cuzzoni refused to sing the aria 'Falsa imagine', whereupon Handel tackled her. 'Oh! Madame (said he) je scais bien que Vous etes une véritable Diablesse: mais je Vous ferai sçavoir, moi, que, je suis Beelzebub le Chef des Diables.' [Oh, Madam, I well know that you are a true devil: but I'll have you know that I am Beelzebub, chief of the devils.] With this he took her up by the waist, and, if she made any more words, swore that he would fling her out of the window.'

Cuzzoni apparently complied, and she was such a success in the theatre that tickets were changing hands at exorbitant black market prices and the management had to warn those in the Footmen's Gallery (to which servants and the like were admitted free) to maintain order. Opera fever swamped London. The Academy's finances duly benefited. Bononcini's *Erminia* and Ariosti's *Coriolano* were both staged during this season, but it ended with Handel's *Flavio*, first seen on 14 May 1723, which flagrantly and brilliantly parodied the heroics of *opera seria*.

For the following season, Handel wrote only one opera, but put into it an unusual amount of care. The work was, to give it its full title, *Giulio Cesare in Egitto*. The text was by Haym. Composition began in the summer of 1723, and the opera was first seen on 20 February 1724. It was a tremendous and deserved success. He used more lavish an orchestra in terms of available colours than he had since his time in Rome, including a stage band which plays in Cleopatra's famous aria 'V'adoro, pupille'. But what gives this work its greatness is its combination of a sense of epic with subtle sensualities. *Giulio Cesare* is genuinely grand opera. His finances bolstered by the new work's popularity, Handel moved house, to what is now 25 Brook Street in the West End of London. He was to live there until his death. Besides music for the opera, Handel composed little. In any case, there cannot have been much spare time available for him to do very much more than he already was. There were, however, performances of a new anthem (probably *Let God Arise*) for the King's return to England in January 1724. The

*Handel painted
by Philip Mercier*

A pastel drawing of Faustina Bordoni
by Rosalba Carriera

sixth season began on 31 October 1724 with another opera to a libretto by Haym, *Tamerlano*. It caused much comment because, although the castrato ruled supreme in London's operatic scene, the hero Bajazet was assigned to a tenor, Francesco Borosini. After the first performance, Handel threw much energy into fashioning the work to his satisfaction. He made five versions of the Act I prison scene, and in so doing converted the work into what is now acknowledged to be a masterpiece. Later in the season, on 13 February 1725, a second new opera, again based on words by Haym, was seen: *Rodelinda*. Cuzzoni once more made an extraordinary impact with the public, not least with her costume, which the young of society adopted as the latest fashion and the old dismissed as lacking decorum. The offending dress sounds innocuous enough to us: brown silk trimmed with silver.

Cuzzoni was soon to have a rival in the same company. In their wisdom, the directors of the Academy secured, at the crippling expense of £2,500, the sevices of Faustina Bordoni. Bordoni was, in many respects, Cuzzoni's opposite, an attractive person both visually and in temperament, with an agile voice and apparently an enormous lung capacity which enabled her to sustain a note for far longer than any of her singer-colleagues.

Bordoni's arrival was delayed until May 1726. In the meantime the 1725–6 season was largely filled with revivals, though a new opera, *Scipione*, with a text by Rolli, found its way from manuscript to stage (on 26 March 1726) within ten days. But the financial position of the company was far from healthy, and the Academy's shareholders were asked to provide another influx of cash. Handel's first work for the two star sopranos and Senesino was *Alessandro*. Each of the ladies was carefully given the same number of arias as the other; each had a duet with Senesino (with whom each was in love in the plot); and they sang a duet together. *Alessandro* was yet another glowing success, but Senesino, protesting truthfully or otherwise reasons

Etching of George II by John Faber, based on a painting by Joseph Highmore

of ill-health, cancelled his appearance in the final performance and went back to Italy. Consequently, the opening of the next season, which should have taken place in the autumn of 1726, was delayed. Christopher Rich, manager of the rival Lincoln's Inn Fields Theatre, responded to the gap in London's cultural life with a production of the old favourite, Bononcini's *Camilla*, revised to include an acidic prologue that referred to Handel's increasingly mutually hostile sopranos and the unreliability of his castrato.

But in January 1727 the triumvirate was back in action in Handel's latest offering, *Admeto*. The German flautist-composer Quantz, while noting the excellence of the work itself, also commented on increasing disruptions from the audience, which had divided itself into two camps, those who supported Cuzzoni and those whose champion was Bordoni. The situation got worse as the months progressed. In June, when Bononcini's *Astianatte* was holding the stage, matters reached crisis point when the singers themselves fought each other on stage. But that potentially ruinous incident was suddenly relegated to the sidelines a few days later when news came of George I's death in Osnabrück.

Fortuitously, just before the King had left London for the last time, Handel had gained his approval for becoming a British citizen. His first commission after naturalization was for four anthems to be sung at George II's Coronation Service. The *Norwich Gazette* reported that the performers at the occasion numbered '40 Voices, and about 160 Violins, Trumpets, Hautboys [oboes], Kettle-Drums and Bass's proportionable; besides an Organ, which was erected behind the Altar.' The proportion of voices to instruments would seem remarkably badly balanced by today's standards. Precautions had to be taken to keep rehearsal times private, such was the interest aroused by the prospect of these large-scale and magnificent works. In the event, according to the Archbishop of Canterbury, the performance itself did not go well.

Meanwhile, London was able to enjoy the services of Senesino and Cuzzoni for another season at the Opera. But Handel's old friend Mary Granville, who had by now become Mrs Pendarves, expressed misgivings about the whole operation. She doubted the integrity of the directors, who were squabbling amongst themselves, and noted that many subscribers were not renewing their commitment. Nevertheless the 1727–8 season brought three new offerings from Handel: *Riccardo I, Re d'Inghilterra*, *Siroe* (which received nineteen performances), and *Tolomeo*, which was dedicated to the Earl of Albermarle.

But then the arrival of popular competition proved mortally wounding to the Academy. At Lincoln's Inn Fields Theatre, *The Beggar's Opera*, a satirical work based on old ballad tunes set to lyrics by John Gay and arranged by Pepusch, tackled issues closer at hand than the apparently remote, idealized subjects of *opera seria*. Corruption, society, politics, taste were all victims, and the piece closed with a sharp parody of *opera seria's* convention of ending suddenly and usually untenably in happy mood, all parties reconciled. Handel's audience figures duly suffered dramatically, and a performance at the Haymarket of *Admeto* on 1 June 1728 proved to be the swansong of the Royal Academy in its first manifestation.

THE SECOND ACADEMY AND THE ENGLISH OPERA

B ut it was not long before Handel, always an obstinate fighter, launched another ambitious show. Lord Bingley granted Heidegger £2,200 for the season and Handel £1,000 per opera (his or not) for the new venture. In addition a budget of £4,000 was allocated to pay the singers, of which each of the two principals would receive £1,000. Handel and three representatives of the subscribers went to Italy to recruit them. Details of the journey remain vague, but Handel certainly visited Naples and Rome and perhaps Siena. He diplomatically avoided visiting his old Roman patron Cardinal Colonna in Rome because the Jacobite Pretender to the throne was a guest at the time. Among the singers he signed up were Antonio Maria Bernacchi, who the *Daily Journal* said was 'esteem'd the best Singer in Italy'; Antonio Margherita Merighi, described as a 'Counter Tenor'; Anna Maria Strada, possessed of a 'Treble Voice'; Annibal Pio Fabri, a tenor, together with his wife; Signor Bartoldi, 'a very fine Treble Voice'; and Johann Gottfried Riemschneider, a bass from Hamburg. Mrs Pendarves later gave balanced assessments of each singer after seeing them in Handel's latest opera *Lotario*, performed after only two weeks' preparation, which opened in December 1729. 'La Strada', she wrote particularly memorably, 'is the first woman; her voice is without exception fine, her manner perfection, but her person *very bad*, and she makes *frightful mouths*.' *Lotario* was not a critical success; Rolli in particular hated it, but Mrs Pendarves felt able to defend it as 'too good for the vile taste of this town', which was still enthused by *The Beggar's Opera*. It was too much a genuinely serious *opera seria*, so Handel responded with something lighter, *Partenope*, a work which deliberately pokes fun at the old form. It contains much incidental battle music and the like, and when the hero and the heroine (who is disguised as a man) agree to fight stripped to the waist, the work takes on an air of suggestive farce. The ploy, however, did not work and the season was not successful. Bernachi failed to achieve Senesino's success, so Handel plotted once more to secure the latter's services and to find a new soprano. Senesino was eventually lured by the enormous fee of 1,400 guineas, and when the new season opened on 3 November 1730 he immediately had great success with the revival of a much revised version of *Scipione*.

On 16 December Handel's mother died in Halle, but Handel had no time to make any consolatory visits to the parental home, though he was clearly distraught, as a letter to his brother-in-law Michael Michaelsen made clear. Instead, he heroically continued work on the next opera, *Poro*, finishing Act II in one week. The librettist this time was Metastasio; but Handel attempted to shift the balance of the original plot from the lofty to the personal. Senesino, of course, was given the best aria, 'Dov'è? Si affretti'. This season also saw *Rinaldo* and *Rodelinda* revived, and extra performances were added at the end of it to compensate for its late start.

In the meantime Bononcini, Handel's old colleague, had caused a public stir by claiming to be the composer of a piece at the Academy of Ancient Music (a club for professionals) which was discovered by Bernard Gates, Master of the Children of the Chapel Royal, to be by Lotti. That was the hot gossip; but elsewhere more serious compromises of what we would regard as a composer's rights were occurring. At Lincoln's Inn Fields John Rich mounted the first public performance of *Acis and*

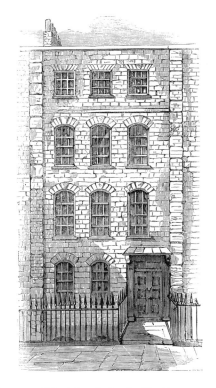

25 Brooke Street, London – Handel's residence

Galatea, the pastoral serenata composed for Cannons years before, without Handel's involvement or prior knowledge.

The following season began on 15 January 1732 with the bass Antonio Montagna making his debut at the King's Theatre in another adaptation from Metastasio, *Ezio*, which was not a huge success. Then came a revival of the now well-established *Giulio Cesare* and on 15 February yet another new opera, *Sosarme*, with its original recitatives drastically cut. Though that compromised the comprehensibility of the work, it succeeded nevertheless. English audiences' chief priority was obviously the aria.

But on Handel's forty-seventh birthday, 23 February 1732, an event happened which was to have far-reaching consequences. Viscount Percival's diary for that day records that at the Music Club the King's Chapel boys 'acted the *History of Hester*, writ by Pope and composed by Hendel'. A manuscript copy of the work concerned, *Esther*, tells us that the piece was also privately performed at the Crown and Anchor tavern in the Strand, where the Chapel Royal children were joined by voices from the choirs of St James's and Westminster who 'join'd in Chorus's, after the Manner of the Ancients, being placed between the Stage and the Orchestra.' Oratorio had arrived in London. Princess Anne asked for a performance at the Haymarket with action, but in the meantime a public performance in the Great Room of York Buildings was planned by person or persons unknown. Handel quickly made substantial revisions and emendations for the Haymarket performance on 2 May 1732. There was lavish scenery but no action, in response to the intervention of the Bishop of London. Some of the additions were lifted from earlier works (*La Resurrezione*, the *Ode on the Birthday of Queen Anne*, the Coronation Anthem *Zadok the Priest*); others were original. The continuo section was particularly large. There were six performances and Handel made a more than healthy sum from them. But for the moment *Esther* appeared to be a one-off work.

Meanwhile a new company, English Opera, which was instigated by Thomas Arne, the father of the composer, his eponymous son, John Frederick Lampe and Henry Carey, staged *Acis and Galatea* again without the composer's cooperation. Handel this time reacted quickly, with a hybrid piece made from combining music from the earlier *Aci, Galatea e Polifemo* with that from the Cannons serenata. One or two new numbers had to be written, but the labour involved was not very much. One oddity about the performance is that it was bilingual. The Italian soloists sang in Italian, the English ones in English, and the chorus had to tackle both languages. Again the work was not acted, but performed on a suitably pastoral set. The gesture having been made, Handel turned once again to what was still his first love, Italian opera.

The 1732–3 season began with a revival of *Alessandro*, with Senesino repeating the role he had created in 1726. Strada and Gismoni were preferred to Faustina and Cuzzoni – no doubt they were easier to deal with – and Montagna sang the role of Clito. The first night was a success, but not the second. It coincided with the staging by the English Opera of a minor work by, of all people, John Christopher Smith the younger, called *Teraminta* and set in exotic Cuba. At the time, Smith was just twenty and a prized pupil of Handel. He also provided a work called *Ulysses* later in the English Opera's season; in addition the rival company staged Lampe's *Amelia*, Arne's burlesque *The Opera of Operas* and the same composer's *Rosamond*.

Clearly, the situation for Handel was becoming serious. In December 1732 Aaron Hill, who by now had quitted the theatre, wrote to Handel encouraging him to explore the possibility of producing an English opera himself. Handel ignored the plea and continued to plough the operatic furrows he knew.

As it happened, Handel's next new opera, following a revival of *Tamerlano*, was one nowadays acknowledged to be a masterpiece. In *Orlando* the composer's concern with dramatic momentum and, importantly, psychological insights, are paramount. Accepted baroque patterns and structures are compromised. Predictability flies out of the window.

MORE RIVALRY – THE OPERA OF THE NOBILITY

*O*rlando opened on 27 January 1733, but soon Handel was up against something else: a new company which was hell-bent on recruiting Senesino (actually a prime mover of the project) and others of Handel's singers. The directors included many of Handel's old allies, Lord Burlington among them. Indeed, five had been on the board of the original Academy. The company, based at Lincoln's Inn Fields, we know as the Opera of the Nobility, though in its own time it had different names. Eventually the two rival groups were both to come to grief.

For the moment, Handel ploughed on regardless, and composed another oratorio, *Deborah*, given at the King's Theatre on 17 March 1733 by a large ensemble of nearly a hundred people, twenty-five of whom were singers. It was a piece that had been rather quickly thrown together from earlier music: the *Brockes Passion*, some of the Chandos Anthems, two of the Coronation Anthems, and some Italian arias. Senesino was still officially Handel's, and duly sang in the ostensibly new oratorio. The performance, however, brought hostile reaction, not least because Handel's confidence was so high that he felt able to charge his audience twice the price that he would normally ask for an opera performance. Moreover, subscribers – holders of the silver tickets that guaranteed them free entry to operas – were at first refused entry altogether. Only brute force got them into the theatre in the end.

This incident clearly did not help Handel's reputation very much, and nor, apparently, his health. The stigma endured. More than a year later, in December 1734, an anonymous person was to write: 'I don't pity Handell in the least, for I hope this mortification will make him a human creature; for I am sure before he was no better than a brute . . . '. But in the summer of 1733 an invitation to take part in the revival in Oxford of the so-called 'Publick Act', a degree-giving

Handel conducting, from a rare contemporary print

ceremony, offered Handel a chance to improve his standing once more. *Deborah*, *Esther* and a new oratorio, *Athalia*, were each to be performed twice in the Sheldonian Theatre in Oxford, as well as the *Utrecht Te Deum and Jubilate*, certain anthems, and a selection of arias. In the event, *Athalia*'s première had to be postponed for a day, since the degree ceremony on 9 July overran.

The theatre was packed, despite objections to Handel's presence in Oxford by a racist minority. *Athalia*, based on Racine, was a conspicuous success as a drama, not least because of its tragic heroine. One revolutionary feature was that its Overture was cast in the Italian form, fast-slow-fast, instead of the traditional French form derived from

Lully, slow-fast-slow. Handel indicated precisely which continuo instruments should accompany where, and the scoring as a whole was unprecedented in its range of colours. We are not sure whether Handel was actually offered a doctorate, but in the event he appears not to have come away with one 'because I was overwhelmingly busy', according to one fragment of a letter printed in an eighteenth-century source. However, he did reap considerable financial reward – reputedly more than £2,000 – from the performances associated with his visit.

Senesino, dismissed by Handel, had transferred his allegiance to the Opera of the Nobility, along with Montagnana, Bertolli and Gismondi, in June 1733. Cuzzoni was to follow her illustrious colleagues in April 1734. Handel and Heidegger had to react quickly in order to engage new artists and find new repertoire in time for the following season. They lured Durastante back from Italy and signed two castrati, Carlo Scalzi and Giovanni Carestini. *Ottone* was revived and supplemented with two operas by other men, but with recitatives by Handel inserted. These were *Semiramide*, most of which was written by Leonardo Vinci, and *Cajo Fabricio*, whose principal author was Handel's old friend, Hasse. The bit seems to have been firmly between Handel's teeth. He opened his season two months before the Opera of the Nobility, timing it to coincide with the King's birthday on 30 October. The entire court went to the opera that night. But the next evening drew adverse comment about some of the new singers, Carestini and Durastante apart. 'All old scrubs', wrote Lady Bristol with rude candour.

Ottone's revival had nevertheless been supported by the royal family. That advantage was tempered by the fact that the Prince of Wales openly offered his house in the Royal Gardens in Pall Mall for a rehearsal of the Opera of the Nobility's first première, Nicola Porpora's *Arianna in Nasso*. Even so, Handel's first new opera in 1734, *Arianna in Creta*, was well received. It ran for seventeen performances, and Carestini was encouragingly singled out for particular praise. Subsequently, a pamphlet called *Harmony in an Uproar* was produced and widely circulated in Handel's support – a timely reply to a vitriolic and, by today's standards, blatantly libellous invective against Handel which had appeared in the journal *The Craftsman* the year before. And he still had the allegiance of the King, the Queen and his pupil Princess Anne to rely upon, even if the Prince of Wales was wobbling.

The memoirs of the dissolute Lord Hervey paint a grim picture of the Prince of Wales's hostility towards Handel, but in fact his testimony to that effect is unique. Accounts for the Prince of Wales's household suggest a far more equitable situation. In the 1733–4 season, for instance, both companies were given £250, and though the Nobility benefited exclusively in the next two seasons, from 1736–7 donations to Handel resumed and continued thereafter until 1744. It should not be ignored, moreover, that the Prince was always a regular member of Handel's audiences.

In March 1734, Princess Anne married William of Orange, and her music teacher duly provided the wedding anthem (*This is the day*) and, for the day before, a serenata, *Il Parnasso in Festa*, which was staged at the King's Theatre. Most of the music for the serenata was lifted directly from *Athalia*. Porpora, at the Nobility, attempted to upstage Handel with an oratorio in Italian, *Davide e Bersabea*, but to little effect. Mrs Pendarves thought the rival offering 'not equal to Mr. Handel's oratorio of *Esther* or *Deborah*', and noted that 'To have words of piety made use of only to introduce good music, is reversing what it ought to be . . .'. Meanwhile, Handel ended his season with revivals of *Sosarme* and a much revised and expanded version of *Il Pastor Fido*. Then came what must have been an unexpected blow for the composer. Heidegger's contract with him came to an end and the manager chose to re-let the theatre to the Opera of the Nobility, purely on commercial grounds. Handel approached John Rich, who had invested his profits from *The Beggar's Opera* in the building of a new Theatre Royal at Covent Garden, designed by Edward Shepherd, the architect who had completed the house at Cannons for the Duke of Chandos. The theatre, with its apron stage, Handel deemed eminently suitable for both opera and oratorio, and Rich agreed to alternate his own plays with Handel's work. Handel took time off to visit Tunbridge Wells to take the waters, but by 12 August he was already at work on his latest opera, *Ariodante*.

Even so, the Opera of the Nobility, with London's best theatre at their disposal, were now established in the driving seat, and they would appear to have clinched their triumph when they engaged the legendary castrato Carlo Broschi, otherwise known as Farinelli, from Italy. Charles Burney extolled Farinelli's talents thus: '. . . by the natural formation of his lungs, and artificial oeconomy [sic] of breath, he was able to protract to such a length as to excite incredulity even in those who had heard him; who, though unable to detect the artifice, imagined him to have had the latent help of some instrument by which the tone was continued, while he renewed his powers by respiration.' Farinelli was the expected success on his debut in Hasse's and his (Farinelli's) brother Riccardo Broschi's joint opera, *Artaserse*. Burney reports extraordinary scenes on stage as Senesino, playing the tyrant in whose chains the hero had been bound, ran over to embrace Farinelli after the latter had sung one aria particularly affectingly.

Handel had little to rival this, but at least there was something. A new singer, the tenor John Beard, was warmly received, while in his next three operas he daringly used the services of the dancer Marie Sallé and her troupe. Sallé caused some consternation among the more moralistic members of the audience with her risqué dress. 'She has dared to appear without pannier, skirt or bodice, and with her hair down', wrote one scandalized journalist. Gossip about her offstage activities abounded. For Sallé Handel revised *Il pastor fido* yet again, adding dance music and composing a French-style opera-ballet called *Terpsichore* to precede it. He then revived *Arianna* and concocted a pasticcio, *Oreste*, from his own material.

January 1735 was the time chosen for the opening of his new opera, *Ariodante*, the second of his works based on Ariosto. He was thus able to steal a march of a whole month on the Nobility's second offering, *Polifemo*. *Ariodante* was not heroic, but gentle and reflective. Burney was not entirely happy with it; he berated its 'monotonously happy' first act as well as the new bass, Gustavus Waltz, with whom Handel had been obliged to replace Montagnana. And Farinelli still ruled the roost, as an account of a benefit concert he gave relates. To say that he was idolized is an understatement. So, despite yet another added attraction Handel provided in his oratorios – performances, with himself as soloist, of organ concertos (a practice he seems already to have started in 1733 with *Esther*) – audiences neglected him.

Johann Mattheson in an engraving by Christian Fritzsch

Typically, he responded with a masterpiece. *Alcina* opened at Covent Garden on 16 April 1735. Mrs Pendarves was mightily impressed, and the King and Queen gave it their enthusiastic support. *Alcina* proved to be Handel's last great success on the opera stage, its heroine a remarkable, intense figure, a ruthless sorcerer whose desertion by her powers and her kingdom yet turns her into a moving character. *Alcina* also has passages of ballet, but Sallé apparently overplayed her role, choosing to danced dressed as Cupid. Males dressed as females were acceptable at the time, but not *vice versa*. She promptly left England for Paris after her not altogether enthusiastic reception. The castrato Carestini also left when *Alcina* finished its run, leaving Handel without a credible rival to Farinelli. He announced on 20 May 1735 that the following season would be of 'Concerts of Musick', but 'no Opera's'. Depressed, he turned down Johann Mattheson's request sent from Hamburg for his autobiography.

The Decline of Handelian Opera

On 28 July Handel wrote a letter, which still survives, to Charles Jennens, a rich, eccentric and overbearing author with whom Handel had probably been acquainted since the 1720s, saying that he had received the text for an oratorio which had given him 'a great deal of Satisfaction.' The libretto might well have been that for *Saul*, though in fact Handel did not set that text until several years afterwards. Meanwhile, the composer also attended the Opera of the Nobility; he had cause to gloat quietly, for the company was also proving unable to engage wide public sympathy.

The tenor, John Beard

Handel's next important task was the composition of *Alexander's Feast*, a setting of the *Ode to St Cecilia* written by Dryden in 1697, with the words adapted for Handel by the author Newburgh Hamilton. The work was infused with Handel's wide dramatic experience, and was coloured with a startlingly rich instrumentation. Its first performance, with the two sopranos Strada and Cecilia Young (shortly to become Mrs Arne), the young tenor Beard and a bass called Mr Erard, was a popular success. Two years later, it was printed in full score by John Walsh, something that had rarely happened to a work of such proportions until then, and Handel was handsomely paid for the honour – £105 as opposed to the usual fee of twenty-five guineas for an opera, twenty guineas for an oratorio. What Walsh did not print was the plethora of extras included in performance: a Concerto Grosso in C (today known as the Concerto in *Alexander's Feast*) and three other concertos, two of them for organ. An Italian cantata written for Strada, *Cecilia, vogli un squardo*, was included with the printed ode.

A royal wedding was on the cards in 1736. The Prince of Wales, whose support of the Opera of the Nobility had helped that company secure its supremacy, was to marry Augusta, Princess of Saxe-Gotha. Handel, never one to miss a chance, had the idea of composing a wedding opera. The resulting work was *Atalanta*, a pastoral tale designed specifically to flatter the Prince. For its performance, the male soprano Gioacchino Conti was imported from Italy; Strada co-starred with him. The work, with its elaborate final scene including fireworks, succeeded as intended, and helped lure the Prince of Wales over to Handel's own cause. Nevertheless, there were those who were heard to mutter that it was the same all over again, that the piece lacked variety.

In the summer of 1736 Handel appears to have rested somewhere in the country. But the success of *Atalanta* gave him new heart, and it helped his morale even more when the Prince of Wales commanded a revival of his wedding piece for the following season. To maintain the flavour of celebration, at the revival of *Alcina* which opened the 1736–7 season on 6 November the royal box remained specially decorated. Meanwhile, Mrs Pendarves remarked on the state of the Nobility in a letter to her sister; 'Merighi with no sound in her voice . . . Montagnana who roars as usual...dull operas, such as you almost fall asleep at . . .'. Clearly, she knew which camp she was supporting.

Handel had prepared two new works in the autumn of 1736, *Arminio* and *Giustino,* but their first runs, which began at Covent Garden on 12 January and 16 February respectively, did not reveal them to be enough, even with Conti and the new alto Domenico Annibali, to put his company back in the lead. Nevertheless, Farinelli's star at the Nobility was beginning to fade, so his company came up with a new idea to attract punters: comic interludes between acts. *Il Giocatore* was seen for the first time within Hasse's *Siroe* on 1 January 1737, and became the first Italian comic opera heard in London. Even so, audience figures were continuing to fall fast everywhere.

Handel's responding ploy was to advertise performances of opera throughout Lent, on the Wednesday and Friday of each week. But to no avail: a ban was imposed, so that he was forced to resort to revivals of *Alexander's Feast* and the oratorios *Esther* and *Deborah* instead, along with new concertos for organ and other instruments. Also promised was a complete rewrite of his very first oratorio, dating from his sojourn in Rome. *Il trionfo del Tempo e del Disinganno*, written in 1707, became *Il trionfo del Tempo e della Verità*. Later, this in turn was to be metamorphosed into his last work, *The Triumph of Time and Truth*.

Immediately after Easter the pace at Covent Garden was as frantic as it had ever been. There was a pasticcio, mostly with music by Vinci, called *Dido*; on 4 May *Giustino* resumed the stage; on 18 May *Berenice,* which Handel had composed over the previous Christmas and New Year periods, received its first performance. But these

Farinelli (Carol Broschi) the Italian castrato singer

events probably took place without Handel's assistance. He suffered what seems to have been a stroke on 13 April.

Berenice ran for only four nights, but at least Handel's company outlasted the Nobility, which closed for good on 11 June after Farinelli, who was still its major attraction, had developed a cold and withdrawn. The great castrato was subsequently lured by King Philip v of Spain to his service. His only duty was to sing the same three arias each day as a cure for the King's melancholy.

We are not sure, but Handel might have been well enough to direct a royal command performance of *Alexander's Feast* on 25 June. The time had come, however, for a break from both the artistic and economic strain. He repaired to the baths at Aix-la-Chapelle to take a six-week cure for paralysis, which seems to have been remarkably effective. Meanwhile, back in England, not only Farinelli but also Senesino and Cuzzoni had left the Nobility. Conti and Strada did not sing for Handel again after *Berenice*. A radical change in London's musical life was in the air.

ORATORIO RESURGENS

While at Aix, Handel had had time to think. During his fall from operatic grace he had never really risked personal financial ruin. Income from commissions, his royal pension and the fact that he had always been a beneficiary rather than a personal investor saw to that. But London demonstrably had no room for two opera companies. It did not help Handel's cause that he was, by nature, an obstinate man, cocksure of his own abilities and unwilling to change course. Yet he already had evidence of success with his oratorios, wherein, perhaps, lay the link between the splendid state music for which he had become best known and the personal, and for contemporaneous audiences possibly even over-refined, drama of his operas. If oratorio brought with it another danger, of the accusation of blasphemy, he had the additional fallbacks of the slightly vague genre of the pastoral ode or of the relatively sure investment of instrumental music, which could be published and sold to amateurs.

Handel returned to London in November, 1737 to find that John Rich was staging John Lampe's burlesque *The Dragon of Wantley* at Covent Garden and filling the theatre night after night with it. The work had a specific target: Handel's own *Giustino*. Down the road at the King's Theatre, Haymarket, Heidegger, now going it virtually alone financially, opened with the pasticcio *Arsace*. A certain Signor Caffarelli was his replacement for Farinelli, and Giovanni Pescetti was engaged as Heidegger's house composer for the season. But less than two weeks after returning, Handel had been recruited by Heidegger to write two operas and one pasticcio and to act as musical director for the sum of £1,000. He immediately began work on a new opera, *Faramondo*. Then, on 20 November, Queen Caroline died. All work in the theatre ceased.

Handel responded to what was genuinely a personal tragedy for him with the extended funeral anthem, *The Ways of Zion do Mourn*. This is an impressive piece, quoting an old motet by the German composer Jacob Handl, *Ecce quomodo moritor justus*, which was still sung at Lutheran funerals, as well as a Lutheran chorale melody. There is also a palpable influence from earlier English church music. What the work lacks is any operatic traits, for that would have been inappropriate for the occasion.

Nevertheless, just one week after the Queen's funeral, on Christmas Eve 1737, *Faramondo* was complete, and on St Stephen's Day, 26 December, Handel began the composition of yet another new opera, *Serse*. One day's holiday was apparently plenty. *Faramondo* reached the stage on 3 January 1738, with a highly rated newcomer, the soprano Elisabeth Duparc, known as 'La Francesina', among the cast. At Covent Garden, however, *The Dragon of Wantley* was still pulling in the crowds, and *Faramondo* closed after just eight nights, despite being greatly admired by the likes of Burney. Handel, anxious to recoup losses, advertised the printed score to potential subscribers through his publisher John Walsh, to be made available by 4 February. One month later, the printed score of *Alexander's Feast*, already subscribed to, was ready, and it was quickly followed by the songs from *Alessandro Severo*, a work which Handel had cobbled together from earlier operas, adding new recitatives and an overture, and which ran for six nights from 25 February.

But Handel's finances were still being stretched, so, encouraged by his friends, on 28 March at the King's Theatre he staged a benefit concert at which was given a strange mixture of pieces from *Esther* and *Athalia* and some Italian arias, all in the context of a distilled version of *Deborah*. Zadok the Priest and an organ concerto completed the programme, which raised a considerable sum. Mainwaring estimates £1,500, though others claimed only £800. Handel learned some lessons from this exercise. The profit was equivalent to two operas and a pasticcio at Heidegger's rates. He was popular, as the erection in April of Louis François Roubiliac's marble statue of him in Vauxhall Gardens, then a unique tribute to a still-living artist, testified. (The statue can now be seen in the Victoria and Albert Museum.) And oratorio, even a hotch-potch like this, clearly did not dissuade audiences.

Just a fortnight after the benefit evening his new opera, *Serse*, failed, despite the many obviously fine qualities that have ensured its success in our own times. The cast was good, the work contained an element of what should have been audience-attracting comedy, and there was that arresting opening aria, 'Ombrai mai fu', sung by the hero in praise of a tree, which in a later, more sentimental century metamorphosed into Handel's *Largo*. *Serse*'s failure was critical. On 26 July Heidegger advertised in the *Daily Post* that the following season's subscription series was cancelled, and all monies would be returned upon application.

Handel, however, was already hard at work on a new venture, the composition of the oratorio *Saul*, whose libretto it was that Charles Jennens may well have sent him three years before. The working manuscript shows the determined struggle he had with the piece. In September he laid it aside to begin work on yet another opera, *Imeneo*. Jennens had paid him a visit, and was dismayed to find him preoccupied with what he, Jennens, considered futile 'maggots': a new organ, a 'carillon' (bells played with a harpsichord-like keyboard) as a special effect for *Saul*, and what he deemed to be an irrelevant Hallelujah chorus for the end of the oratorio. (At Jennens' typically arrogant but, in truth, justified behest, Handel later placed the chorus at the end of Act I.) *Saul* was duly finished after Jennens' visit.

The new work drew heavily on already existing music, both Handel's and others'. But experiment in dramatic form was what primarily preoccupied the composer, and after he had finished *Saul* he quickly sought to consolidate what he had learnt and to push ahead further by writing a new oratorio immediately. At first called *Moses' Song, Israel in Egypt* also exploited other sources. Music by Francesco Urio (who also appears in *Saul*), Stradella and Dionigi Erba finds its way into this work. The *Funeral Ode* rejected from *Saul* became Part I, the *Lamentations of the Israelites for the Death of Joseph*. The emphasis in *Israel in Egypt* is on the impact of the choral movements rather than on orchestral effect. Moreover, the text comes directly from the Bible, and individuals are less significant than whole nations. *Saul* and *Israel in Egypt* can be seen, then, as direct opposites of each other.

A pottery bust of Handel fashioned in the composer's lifetime

Armed with these pieces and with *Alexander's Feast* and *Il trionfo del Tempo e della Verita*, Handel hired the King's Theatre for twelve performances of oratorio, spread through the first half of 1739. *Saul*, which opened on 16 January and was performed with several new organ concertos through its run, was a success. For it, Handel borrowed from the Duke of Argyll a set of 'the largest kettle-drums in the tower', according to Lord Wentworth. *Alexander's Feast* followed on 17 February, with three extra concertos, and then on 3 March *Il trionfo*, again with 'several Concerto's on the Organ and other Instruments', according to the *Daily Post*. On 20 March Handel gave a charity performance of *Alexander's Feast* for the Fund for the Support of Decayed Musicians and their Families (now the

Handel by
Jan van der Banck

Royal Society of Musicians). *Israel in Egypt* came last in the season, on 4 April. It was a failure, so the second performance was leavened with extracts sung by 'La Francesina' from *Athalia* and the Italian arias that had earlier been added to *Esther.* An anonymous letter in the *Daily Post* enthused over the piece so much that Handel tried for a third performance, attended by the Prince and Princess of Wales. Another eulogistic letter subsequently appeared in the *Daily Post*, but the season still ended rather tamely. Adjustment to *Israel in Egypt* was needed, and eventually, in the 1750s, the original Part I was jettisoned. For his next offering Handel, disappointed, resorted to another operatic pasticcio, *Jupiter in Argos,* which ran for two nights only and then disappeared.

Meanwhile, Walsh had been busy publishing Handel's accumulated corpus of instrumental music. On 28 September 1738 he advertised an edition of six harpsichord and organ concertos made from the composer's autograph and corrected by him, in response to a pirated edition that was doing the rounds. 'Seven Sonat's, or Trio's, for two Violins, or German Flutes, and a Bass. Opera Quinta' followed in January 1739. Some of these were reworkings of the overtures to the Chandos Anthems. Later, protected by a new Privilege of Copyright dated 31 October, came an impressive collection of brand new pieces, 'Twelve Grand Concerto's, in Seven Parts, for four Violins, a Tenor, a Violincello, with a Thorough-Bass for the Harpsichord' Op.6. These were composed at white heat in just over a month, from September to October 1739. They follow the Corellian line of development, rather than the Venetian, virtuosic school of Vivaldi and Albinoni, or indeed the individualistic colourings and revolutionary forms of Bach's Brandenburg Concertos. Some ideas come from the German composer Gottlieb Muffat's keyboard suites, *Componimenti Musicali*, a collection also trawled for Handel's *Ode for St Cecilia's Day*, a setting of Dryden's verse composed shortly before the concertos. Other ideas in these concertos can be traced to

Domenico Scarlatti's *Essercizi per cembalo*, published in 1738 and 1739.

For the new season, Handel hired the smaller theatre at Lincoln's Inn Fields from John Rich. This time, he opened with the new *Ode* and extracts from *Alexander's Feast* on St Cecilia's Day itself, 22 November. But there was now a war on with Spain, which caused general depression, and the weather was so cold that the Thames froze. A month later the *Ode* was repeated, with *Acis and Galatea* as the supporting work. Understandably, nobody wanted to venture out of doors. Then some of the singers fell ill, necessitating the cancellation of a repeat performance of *Acis* in the New Year. Handel thus had a little time to set to work on his third oratorio to a text by Jennens. *L'Allegro, il Penseroso ed il Moderato* was based on works by Milton. Despite its apparent contrast to the other music he wrote around this time, Handel succeeded in making light work of composing appropriate music for such a pastoral abstraction. *L'Allegro* was performed five times from 27 February. In between the composer slotted revivals of *Esther*, *Saul* and *Israel in Egypt* – one performance each, and supplemented with concertos from Op. 6. That set was duly published on 21 April, complete with a subscribers' list of one hundred names, including royalty, impresarios, the Ladies Concert in Lincoln and the Monday night Musical Society of the Globe Tavern in Fleet Street. But this success did not of itself resolve Handel's continuing artistic and financial dilemmas.

Handel again went abroad in the summer of 1740. We know he played the organ at Haarlem on 9 September, but otherwise his movements are undocumented. On his return, he eschewed oratorio once more, and resumed work on his as yet unfinished new opera, *Imeneo*, begun two years before. This he completed on 10 October, and on 27 October began yet another, *Deidamia*, to a libretto by Rolli. Once more he hired the theatre at Lincoln's Inn Fields and opened the 1740–1 season with a scenic production of the serenata *Il Parnasso in Festa* on 8 November, following it with the première of

Imeneo on 22 November. William Savage, who had been a treble soloist in *Alcina* in 1735 and then an alto in *Giustino* in 1737 and *Faramondo* in 1738, sang the bass title role in the new opera. The castrato Giovanni Battista Andreoni was Tirinto. Handel experimented with a simple plot, nearly comic, and with eminently tuneful music, though the third act has a dramatic, feigned 'Mad Scene'. The experiment once again failed. A two-night run was all the opera could command. *Deidamia* also attempted to lighten the seriousness of *opera seria*, and boasted the attraction of a new singer from Italy, Maria Monza. Its instrumentation included the lute, appearing for the last time in an orchestral score. It closed after three performances, and Handel ended the 1740-1 season with performances of *L'Allegro*, *Il Parnasso*, *Acis* and *Saul*. He was not to write another opera for the rest of his life.

Rumour had it that he was tired and despondent and, moreover, intended to leave London for good. Indeed, by July 1741 he was composing some light Italian duets, perfect repertoire for a German court. On the other hand, sounder evidence suggests that he was genuinely relieved at having relinquished what must have become a heavy burden.

MESSIAH AND ITS SEQUELS

On 30 July 1741 Thomas Dampier writes of Handel's high spirits. He was busying himself looking at new works received from abroad. Perhaps to help dissuade him from thinking about leaving England, Jennens, as he reported to his friend Edward

Holdsworth on 10 July, tried to tempt him with a proposition for an oratorio. The subject he had in mind was nothing less than the story of the Messiah. But it was an approach to Handel from William Cavendish, Lord Lieutenant in Dublin, inviting the famous composer to take part in a season of oratorio concerts in aid of local charities in that city, which finally set Handel to work on the piece. It was to be heard alongside *L'Allegro*, *Acis*, the *Ode on St Cecilia's Day* and *Alexander's Feast*.

Work began on *Messiah* on 22 August 1741. By 28 August Part I was complete. Part II took until 6 September, and Part III until 12 September. Two more days were spent filling in the inner parts, and all of a sudden one of the greatest and most enduring works of art ever created was finished: twenty-four days of labour in all.

Messiah is a hybrid. Intended, as Jennens put it, as 'a fine entertainment', it was nevertheless the only one of Handel's oratorios to be performed in a church in his lifetime. There is no theatrical drama, only biography and philosophy. Its scheme marks a logical progression from Prophecy through to Resurrection, Ascension and Redemption. Jennens' adaptation, both in his overall planning and in his compression of biblical texts, works brilliantly, so that, unusually, Handel was able to work at the piece from beginning to end without any judicious structural reordering or radical rethinking. It is perhaps better to draw a veil over the legends surrounding the circumstances of its composition. Tales of working so feverishly as to forget about eating (highly unlikely in Handel's case), of tears mingling with ink, of Handel supposedly saying, 'I did think I did see all Heaven before me' are almost certainly apocryphal. There is every cause to think of the work as being composed in a state of sober, quiet thought, such is the restraint shown by the composer when easier, more theatrical solutions were equally possible. Indeed, for the first performance the scoring was simply for strings, continuo and, naturally enough in the chorus 'Glory to God', a trumpet. Oboes and bassoons were added only for the first London performances, doubling the string parts in the choruses.

The balance between the choruses and solos is such that neither is allowed to dominate, and the solo writing itself does not approach the coloratura style of the standard *opera seria* aria. Word painting – where a line or some other musical gesture functions as a sonic onomatopoeia – can be found in many places, but such devices are never permitted to drench the work. There is a degree of self borrowing, notably from the recent Italian duets, which are turned into the choruses 'For unto us a child is born', 'And He shall purify' and 'His yoke is easy'. Other sources include Telemann's collection of solo sacred cantatas *Harmonischer Gottes-Dienst*, which had been published in Hamburg in the 1720s.

The original score for 'My Redeemer liveth', Messiah

Having finished this work so quickly, Handel scarcely paused for breath before sitting down to pen his next oratorio. This was *Samson*, whose first act was finished by Michaelmas Day, 29 September 1741. By the end of October the whole work was done. In contrast to *Messiah*'s emphasis on philosophical contemplation, *Samson* is real cut-and-thrust drama, delighting in the opposition of choruses of Philistines and Israelites, and with a cast of well-defined characters. The libretto was by Newburgh Hamilton, who adapted Milton's *Samson Agonistes* for the purpose, adding odd lines of his own for the arias. Samson himself is a powerfully drawn character, who engages our sympathy and whose situation increases our suspense until, at the eleventh hour, God intervenes. The score is highly colourful, and the borrowings from other composers are numerous. Many are from Giovanni Porta's opera *Numitore*, the work which had opened Handel's first season with the Royal Academy in 1720.

After seeing Galuppi's compilation *Alessandro in Persia* at the King's Theatre on 31 October, Handel left for Dublin with his copyist John Christopher Smith in attendance and all the material he would need. Jennens, informed of Handel's departure, was not pleased to learn that *Messiah*'s première would not be happening in London. Windy conditions meant that Handel had to stay for several days in Chester, where a local singer named Janson, recruited to help check some parts, apparently incurred his wrath by failing to live up to the Chester Cathedral organist's claim that he could read at sight. Eventually, the composer disembarked in Dublin on 18 November, and three days later 'Signiora Avolio, an excellent Singer' also arrived. Handel's *Utrecht Te Deum and Jubilate* were performed in a service in aid of the Mercer's Hospital with Handel himself at the organ. That first appearance seems to have sealed his popularity in Dublin. His reception must have been refreshing after the difficult atmosphere he had had to endure in London. And it was not simply novelty value either: Dublin was

The Music Hall, Fishamble, Dublin where the Messiah was first performed

a sophisticated musical city. Handel's friend, the violinist Matthew Dubourg, was Master of the State Music, and around this period the town boasted associations with many noted composers, Geminiani, Thomas and Michael Arne, Lampe and Castrucci among them.

Handel's season opened at the New Music Hall in Fishamble Street on 21 December with *L'Allegro, il Penseroso ed il Moderato* and the usual smattering of concertos as extras. The composer wrote to Jennens of its immense success and of a promise he had immediately been given for an extension to the originally proposed six nights of his season. *L'Allegro* was repeated on 13 January 1742; on 20 January *Acis and Galatea* and the *Ode for St Cecilia's Day* were programmed; *Esther* (with the usual additions) came on 30 January and *Alexander's Feast* began a second series of concerts on 13 February. A concert version of the opera *Imeneo* (described as 'a new Serenata called *Hymen*') with Thomas Arne's sister, Susanna Cibber, singing was heard on 24 March. Cibber's voice was not universally admired – Burney described it as 'a thread' – but she was a fine actress and apparently charmed Handel considerably.

Thomas Arne's sister, Susanna Cibber, who sang in the first performance of the Messiah

Cibber also took part in the first performance of *Messiah*, which was given, according to the *Dublin Journal* of 27 March, 'For Relief of the Prisoners in the several Gaols, and for the Support of Mercer's Hospital in Stephen's Street, and of the Charitable Infirmary on the Inns Quay'. First scheduled for Monday 12 April, the performance was postponed until the following day. Ladies were requested to come 'without Hoops', those giant frames that held out their dresses, in order to make more room. A public rehearsal whetted appetites and caused comment that it was the greatest piece of music that had ever been heard. The performance itself was equally rapturously received. During it, the Reverend Dr Delany, a friend of the Cathedral's mentally unstable Dean, the author Jonathan Swift, reputedly stood up after Cibber had sung 'He was despised' and uttered the immortal line 'Woman, for this be all thy sins forgiven!'.

In May there was a performance of *Saul*, and on 3 June a repeat of *Messiah*. An evening in which Cibber joined her sister-in-law Cecilia Arne in solos and duets by Handel, and a visit to the Smock-Alley Theatre to see Garrick in *Hamlet* concluded the composer's tour. In the second week of August Handel departed, a very popular man indeed.

Back in England, Handel found that in his absence he had been lavishly and publicly praised by Alexander Pope. Lord Middlesex's latest operatic enterprise was failing dismally; Handel was approached for two new operas, with a fee of 1,000 guineas for the pair, but wrote on 9 September to Jennens that he was anticipating being back in Ireland the following year, lured by the popularity of his oratorio. For the moment, however, he did nothing, apart from turning down one suggestion from Dr Edward Synge, Bishop of Elphin, for a sequel to *Messiah* to be called *The Penitent*, and finishing the score of *Samson*. But by the New Year of 1743 he announced an oratorio season, on the same lines as that in Dublin, at Covent Garden. By 5 February a new Organ

Concerto (Op. 7 No. 2), to be performed at Covent Garden on 18 February within the première of *Samson*, was also completed.

Samson proved a huge success, as even the mealy-mouthed cynic Horace Walpole admitted. (He nevertheless ruthlessly criticized the English singers.) Innovatively, the tenor Beard was cast as the hero. For five more nights *Samson* filled the theatre, and Handel followed this success with six more events, beginning with *L'Allegro e il Penseroso* (but not *Il Moderato*) and continuing with what was announced simply as 'A NEW SACRED ORATORIO' – *Messiah*. Despite a letter signed by 'Philalethes' which appeared in the *Universal Spectator*, severely questioning the propriety of performing sacred oratorio in the theatre – this was a period of new religious stirrings, when Puritanism sometimes featured over-strongly – the performance went ahead. Astonishingly, Jennens, still smarting from the fact that *Messiah* had reached Dublin first, expressed bitter disappointment with the work in a letter to his friend Holdsworth, claiming that Handel wrote it too hastily. He also complained that *Samson* was too full of plagiarisms. On 21 February there was a further letter from the same source to the same recipient, stating that "'tis still in his power by retouching the weak parts to make it fit for a publick performance: & I have said a great deal to him on the Subject; but he is so lazy & so obstinate, that I much doubt the effect.'

Early in May, Handel experienced some kind of physical disorder which affected his thinking and speaking, a return, perhaps, to the illness of some years before. At least the resulting sympathy tempered Jennens' ferocity. The relapse was only temporary, however, and by the next month he was planning a new oratorio. *Semele* had a decidedly secular text, based on a libretto by William Congreve which had earlier been set by the composer John Eccles. Newburgh Hamilton once again helped with the adaption, cutting recitative, inserting choruses, changing arias.

Semele was finished within a month, and Handel was ready to charge headlong into its successor when news came of the significant English and Hanoverian victory over the French in the War of the Austrian Succession at Dettingen, under the personal command of George II. Once again, Handel turned into a patriotic composer for the occasion, setting to work on the *Dettingen Te Deum* and the anthem *The King shall rejoice*, for which he drew material from the Italian composer Francesco Urio.

During the next few months, Handel's public at the King's Theatre was offered a hotch-potch derived from *Alessandro* and called *Roxana, or Alexander in India*, perhaps in place of the new opera he had refused to write for the theatre. It ran for twelve nights, but Mrs Delany, as by then she had become, was not fooled, writing that 'it vexed me to hear some favourite songs mangled'. She and her new husband, however, thoroughly approved of the *Dettingen Te Deum*. That out of the way, Handel began his next oratorio, *Joseph and his Brethren*, for which the Reverend James Miller wrote a rather odd libretto. Handel did his remarkable best with it, but the story omitted some vital detail, and Miller provided little opportunity for the really dynamic drama that occurs when opposite stances are collided.

The year 1744 began with an announcement in the *Daily Post* of a subscription series of twelve concerts, including two new works, the following Lent at Covent Garden. *Semele*, which Jennens later lambasted as 'a baudy Opera', was the first of the new oratorios. Mrs Delany took to it immediately on hearing it rehearsed on 23 January. Her affection for the work only deepened after its première on 10 February, and the more so after another look ten days later. Nevertheless, she readily recognized that there was a considerable body of opinion against it on moral grounds, 'viz. the fine ladies, petit maîtres and *ignoramus's*'. Her clerical husband certainly thought it improper for him to attend so profane a work. Among the cast, 'La Francesina' was apparently singing particularly well.

Samson was revived on 24 February, and then came *Joseph and his Brethren*, which was also fairly successful. The season closed on 21 March with *Saul*, not *Messiah*, as Mrs Delany had hoped. But her disappointment was tempered with glee when, on 3 April, Handel joined a dinner party at her house and played a transcription of *Joseph* to the assembled company. Walsh was publishing keyboard transcriptions of sets of overtures at the time, so the practice of reducing scores and playing them at the keyboard must have been fashionable. Financially, Handel's oratorio enterprise had been successful. By contrast, over at the King's Theatre, Lord Middlesex's operatic enterprise had flopped entirely. One excuse offered was that nobody wanted to hear foreign singers, Catholics to boot, in a time of war with a Catholic country. The opera managers decided not to re-book the King's Theatre for the next winter, so Handel himself stepped in and secured it

George II, King of Great Britain and Ireland and Elector of Hanover

for himself. Come the summer of 1744, he once more prepared to set to work on new pieces. First there was *Semele*'s successor, *Hercules*, to words by the Reverend Thomas Broughton, a far better librettist than Miller. Taking his cues from Sophocles and Ovid, and mixing in a good deal of his own imagination, Broughton cleverly introduced all the human tensions that good drama, whatever the genre, demands. Handel responded with what many scholars regard as the height of achievement in the field of baroque music drama by any composer. At the very same time, however, he was already thinking about a sacred counterpart for *Hercules*. For this project he turned once more to Jennens, and also with apparently genuine humility asked him to point out specifically the passages in *Messiah* which he, Jennens, deemed unsatisfactory. The subject for the new work was the story of Belshazzar, and Handel set it with a keenness rare even for him, beginning work before the words for Act III had even arrived, exhorting Jennens for instalments and almost running out of text after just three weeks' labour. With impeccable manners, he entreated Jennens to sanction certain passages to be cut from his text, even though the original would be printed in full in the word-book, as was the custom. Jennens responded to Handel in his usual way, via a third party: '. . . if he does not mend his manners I am resolv'd to have no more to do with him', he wrote to Holdsworth. Nevertheless, he did his job like the expert and the professional he was.

The new works completed, Handel confidently advertised in the *Daily Post* a subscription season of twenty-four performances, beginning on 3 November and continuing each Saturday until Lent, when Wednesdays and Fridays were the chosen times. There was still opposition to him from the opera camp. Bills were torn down almost as soon as they were put up, and one notorious socialite, Lady Margaret Cecil Brown, deliberately organized parties on the evenings of performances. *Deborah* duly opened on 3 November but a request subsequently appeared in the *Daily Advertiser* for Handel to cancel the following week's performance because 'the greatest Part of Mr. Handel's Subscribers are not in Town'. *Deborah* received one more performance, then came *Semele*, twice, with additions from other works. Audience figures were less than satisfactory. The next performance was the première of *Hercules*, which took place on 5 January 1745. The work was repeated the following week, and then Handel aborted his series with a typically eloquent letter printed in the *Daily Advertiser* on 17 January which managed to explain why without resorting to whingeing complaint, and offering subscribers a seventy-five per cent refund. The next day a reply appeared on behalf of the subscribers, declining the offer. Handel, touched as well as morally obliged, changed his mind and decided to plough on and 'perform what Part of it I can'. Jennens blamed Handel's own mismanagement for his failure, citing the clashes with other events on Saturdays as one reason for poor attendance. In other years, he had stuck to his Lenten routine whether it was Lent or not. On Wednesdays and Fridays there was no rival entertainment in town.

The series resumed on 1 March with *Samson*. *Saul* and *Joseph* were also promised, and the Arnes generously arranged to avoid clashes with their company at Drury Lane. On 27 March 1745, *Belshazzar* was premièred, but to a nearly empty house. It ran for three nights, not the most auspicious beginning for what is now acknowledged as a masterpiece. *Messiah*, which again bore the name *A Sacred Oratorio*, had an even less successful run: just two nights. Obviously still failing to attract a public, after sixteen concerts he again attempted, this time successfully, to abandon the season, afraid of risking the loss of a great deal of money. To recoup some of his losses, he sold the organs used at Covent Garden. It is important to note that the season's failure did not financially ruin him. But he was a businessman as well as a composer, and losing money hurt.

The worries about that and about his reputation brought on another failure in his health, so he took a holiday in June at Exton Hall, the home of the Earl of Gainsborough in Leicestershire. There he put together some music for a performance of Milton's masque *Comus*, which the Earl and his two daughters were to perform, using three newly composed songs with numbers from *Alcina* and *L'Allegro*. Then he left for Scarborough. There, however, Handel did not compose anything. There was a new preoccupation to worry him, as it did the rest of the country. During George II's absence in Hanover the Young Pretender, Bonnie Prince Charlie, landed in Scotland and started to move southward. The English army returned from Flanders and London armed itself against possible attack. At the King's Theatre, a recently engaged resident composer, the young Christoph Willibald Gluck, wrote a patriotic opera called *La Caduta de'giganti* to help national morale. It was not the hoped-for success either musically or sociologically. Subsequently, Handel is supposed to have offered Gluck commiseration and kindly advice.

Meanwhile, however, he was still unwell, 'a good deal disordered in the head', as the Earl of Shaftesbury put it in October. But patriotic gestures were the order of the day, so despite his poor health he managed to put together the *Occasional Oratorio*, borrowing from *Athalia*, *Israel in Egypt*, the new songs for *Comus* and the Concertos Op. 6, as well as material traceable to Telemann and Stradella. The Reverend William Morris was impressed; not so Jennens, who also attacked the librettist, Newburgh Hamilton, with his usual venom.

Then the tide turned in the rebellion of the Bonnie Prince. The Jacobites were at last forced back north after getting as far south as Derby, and by April, with the Loyalists' victory at Culloden, they had been defeated entirely. Handel set to work again on a new oratorio, *Judas Maccabaeus*. This time he also had a new librettist, the Reverend Thomas

Morell, by all accounts a pleasant and sympathetic man. The collaboration was happy, Morrell complaisant. He tells of turning up one day and working *ad libitum*, with the composer throwing ideas and himself supplying text for the chorus 'So fall thy Foes, O Lord'. There are a number of borrowings in the original score, but the celebrated chorus 'See the conqu'ring Hero comes' was composed for the later oratorio *Joshua*, and was added, with its subsequent March, for the revival of *Judas Maccabaeus* in 1750, since when it has remained firmly rooted in the earlier work.

With *Judas Maccabaeus*, Handel for once hit the mood of London perfectly. You did not need a subscription to go and hear it; instead the public simply bought a single ticket and went. London's considerable Jewish population was given its own hero, and partly because of that, the takings were high both at the first performance, on 1 April 1747, and during the run, which ended on 15 April. Next came the oratorio *Alexander Balus*, again with a text by Morrell. This time the story had an Eastern flavour, and Morell provided a libretto of impressive efficiency, even if it did lack a sense of poetic inspiration. Handel responded with a colourful and dramatically vivid score. The role of the chorus was reduced, and the plot had an important love story as distraction from the religious element. The work ended not in triumph, as Morell suggested, but sadly, with Cleopatra 'forgetting and forgot' and a chorus in the minor key.

The final work in what turned out to be a quartet of militaristic and therefore arguably politically motivated oratorios was another setting of words by Morell, *Joshua*. Again the hero is a Jew; again there is a romantic subplot, and again the orchestration – horns and flutes and side-drum as well as trumpets and oboes – was lavish for its time. Before either *Alexander Balus* or *Joshua* were given in public, at the King's Theatre Lord Middlesex mounted a homage to Handel in the form of a cobbled-together 'opera', *Lucius Verus*, consisting entirely of arias taken from 'Mr Handel's favourite Operas'.

Ironically, this hybrid was a considerable success. In all twenty-two performances were given just before and just after Christmas 1747. Although Handel accrued no financial benefit from them, at least the work proved that, whatever tribulations his various theatrical enterprises might have brought him, his music was well liked.

A revival of *Judas Maccabaeus* opened his new season at Covent Garden on 26 February; *Joshua*'s première took place on 9 March and that of *Alexander Balus* on 23 March. In all likelihood the three splendid *Concerti a due cori*, which are scored for antiphonal wind bands and which take music from *Alexander Balus*, *Messiah*, *Belshazzar*, *Ottone*, *Semele*, *Lotario*, *Esther*, the *Occasional Oratorio* and *Partenope*, were given as extras in the intervals. *Judas Maccabaeus* was given six times, *Joshua* four times and *Alexander Balus* thrice. The season was successful, Handel made money, and a pattern was set for subsequent Lenten seasons. Moreover, the hostility with the rival Opera was now becalmed. Handel was even able to borrow Italian singers from them – the soprano Guilia Frasi was particularly favoured – to add to his regular team of English artists. Oratorio had arrived and at last become fashionable. Not only that: it was also seen as morally desirable. Those who heard it would come away better people.

Meanwhile, Handel prepared for the 1749 season by relinquishing the militaristic in favour of the idealistic. *Solomon*, whose libretto is anonymous, depicts a Utopian aspiration towards wisdom, justice, piety and – importantly – prosperity in a lavishly rich court. *Susanna* is its opposite, a gentle near-comedy with an again anonymous text based on the Apocrypha that emphasizes the pastoral side of, by implication, English life, the idyll disturbed only by the awkward lechery of two Elders.

For *Solomon*, which Handel began composing on 5 May, extravagant forces were demanded. Over one hundred voices and instrumentalists were anticipated for its première. Among the best known numbers is the Act III Sinfonia, known with singular

The original score for
the Ouverture to Judas Maccabaeus

inaccuracy with regard to what happens in the plot as 'The Arrival of the Queen of Sheba'. For this, as for other numbers, Handel borrowed material copiously from other composers. *Susanna*'s music is also not without its borrowings – the overture, as the musicologist Franklin B. Zimmerman discovered, comes from John Blow's 1684 Ode for St Cecilia, *Begin the Song*. But it also finds Handel deliberately tackling the direct, simple style of the likes of Arne. He worked hard to capture the vital essence of innocence and easiness in his music. The piece succeeded at its first performance, on 10 February, but not, apparently, subsequently. *Solomon* opened on 17 March, when the mezzo-soprano Signora Galli sang the male title role. Galli also appeared in a single performance of *Messiah*, now given under its proper name, on 23 March. This was

Handel's first performance of the work since 1745. Such was the scale of forces he had contracted for the season that he was obliged to designate full and reduced forces ('*con ripieno*' and '*senza ripieno*') in the score and parts of *Messiah* used on this occasion.

Once again, there was cause for celebration when the War of the Austrian Succession came to its close with the signing of the Treaty of Aix-la-Chapelle in October 1748. In November work began on the erection in Green Park of a huge wooden edifice, designed by Jean-Nicholas Servan (a theatre set designer who was known by the Italianate form of his name, Giovanni Servandoni) and intended to form the base for an extravagant firework display. Peace was officially proclaimed the following February, and Handel received the commission to provide the music for the party. Diligent as ever, he duly sped ahead with composition. On 28 March 1749, the Duke of Montague, in his capacity of Master General of the Ordnance, wrote complaining of Handel's headstrong attitude. The King had only accepted the idea of music accompanying the display because Montague had told him that Handel was thinking of using sixteen trumpets and sixteen French horns. He expressed the hope that there would be 'no fidles'. But Handel had other ideas, and wanted to include strings and to use only a dozen each of the martial brass instruments. The autograph requires nine trumpets, nine horns, twenty-four oboes, twelve bassoons and three pairs of timpani, but Handel appended a note saying that strings should double the oboe and bassoon parts. However, cues for strings in some of the later movements are cancelled; we do not know who eventually got his way. Against Handel's will there was a public rehearsal on 21 April in Vauxhall Gardens which caused a traffic jam but which otherwise was a success, attracting an audience of some 12,000 people. The April issue of *Gentleman's Magazine* reports a logjam lasting three hours on London Bridge. But the event itself, on 27 April, was a disaster. Charles Frederick, 'Comptroller of his Majesty's

Thomas Hudson's 1749 portrait of Handel with the score of Messiah just visible beneath the composer's hand

Fireworks as well as for War as for Triumph', was accused by Servan of having failed in his work; Servan even drew his sword on him. Apart from the rockets, the fireworks were disappointing, lacking variety of colour and with hiatuses between their ignition. And to cap it all, the right-hand pavilion of Servan's structure caught fire. The music, which was probably played before the display while the Royal party toured the structure, was virtually ignored.

Handel was able to use it soon afterwards, however, for a very different purpose. A retired sea captain, Thomas Coram, had been granted a Royal Charter in 1739 for the building of a Foundling Hospital intended to house and educate 'exposed and deserted young children'. Work began in 1742. Support had been forthcoming from many artists as well as the King, who gave £3,000; and in May 1749, Handel offered a concert to raise money for the completion of the chapel. The programme, given on 19 May in the unfinished chapel, included the *Royal Fireworks Music*, pieces from *Solomon* and a new anthem, *Blessed are they that considereth the poor*. A further £2,000 came from the King, while the thousand or so who attended paid some £500 for their tickets. Handel himself remained associated with the Foundling Hospital for the rest of his life. Indeed, the following year he presented the now completed chapel with an organ designed by himself.

But summer was upon him, and so it was down to some serious oratorio composing once more. *Theodora*, written in June and July 1749, is a moving essay about faith. It exhalts the virtues of nobility, loyalty and sacrifice to the extent of the mutual martyrdom of the two lovers, Theodora herself and the Roman soldier, Didymus, whom she converts to Christianity. Once again, the librettist was Morell, and his source was the seventeenth-century writer and scientist Robert Boyle's *The Martyrdom of Theodora and Didymus*. Some time before *Theodora*'s première, Handel received what for

The Green Park edifice built for the fireworks display

him was an unusual commission from John Rich to compose incidental music – songs and dances – for Smollett's play *Alceste*. Though the production, which was to have been designed by Servan, never actually took place, the score was duly written, according to Hawkins as repayment of some unspecified debt. It shows Handel playing the French composer Rameau at his own game, and with marked success. One possible reason for the abandonment of the project was that in February 1750 London was hit by a series of earthquakes. Many people panicked and fled to the country. But on 2 March *Saul* began a new series of Lenten concerts at Covent Garden, and was repeated on 7 March. Two days later came the first of four performances of *Judas Maccabaeus*, and on 16 March *Theodora* received its première, together with a new organ concerto (Op. 7 No. 5). It was given only three times, to small audiences. Morell, in a letter of around 1770, quoted Handel as having admitted that 'the Jews will not come to it (as to *Judas*)

A contemporary firework display
'at White-Hall and on the River Thames on 15 May, 1749'

because it is a Christian story; and the Ladies will not come, because it [is] a virtuous one'. But Handel himself thought some of the music, for instance the Act II chorus 'He saw the lovely youth', to be among his very best, better even than the 'Hallelujah Chorus' in *Messiah*. Later in the season, *Samson* was heard twice (4 and 6 April), while *Messiah* itself closed the season on 12 April.

A further performance of *Messiah* was given on 1 May to inaugurate the Foundling Hospital's new organ. The occasion was apparently gatecrashed, and such was the demand to hear the work that a second performance was hastily arranged for 15 May. Meanwhile, Handel was elected a Governor. Every year afterwards, until Handel died, there was a benefit performance of *Messiah* in aid of the Hospital. Furthermore, he was to leave a copy of the score and parts to the Thomas Coram Foundation so that the tradition might be maintained after his death. Alas, although the Foundation still thrives, the chapel exists no longer. The last surviving location of a public performance of Handel's music in London, it was demolished because of its unsound structure in 1926.

The Foundling Hospital Chapel

Handel now was financially extremely comfortable – it was around this time he bought a large Rembrandt – and in excellent health considering his age. On 1 June he nevertheless took the precaution of making his will, shortly before leaving on his last trip to Germany. A report in the *General Advertiser* of

21 August tells of him receiving serious injuries when his coach overturned between the Hague and Haarlem, but otherwise we do not know precisely where he went or what he did. By Christmas Day he was back in London, and he must have recovered from what had befallen him in the Netherlands, for he wrote to his old friend Telemann thanking him for a copy he had received of a theoretical treatise and promising to send him in return a crate of rare plants (Telemann was an amateur botanist). Much to Handel's distress, a false report, only corrected some time later, came from the bearer of the crate that Telemann had already died.

Meanwhile, in London there was speculation about what, if anything, Handel would next write. In fact in the summer of 1750, between the 28 June and 5 July, he had composed *The Choice of Hercules*, a one-act interlude whose material was plundered largely from the unperformed *Alceste* and which was intended for insertion into *Alexander's Feast*. The Covent Garden season of 1751 began with *Belshazzar* on 22 February, and then came the first of four performances of the revised *Alexander's Feast* on 1 March, once more with a new organ concerto, Op. 7 No. 3, included. *Esther* was revived yet again for a single performance on 15 March, and *Judas Maccabaeus* was given on 20 March. That same day the Prince of Wales died, England was plunged into mourning and the season ended prematurely.

The Choice of Hercules, despite its fine music and lovely scoring, was obviously a hastily conceived stop-gap. Perhaps Handel felt he had not delivered what was required of him, or perhaps with mortality approaching he felt a new sense of urgency. But whatever the reason, he began setting a new text in January 1751, just before the concert season started. Once again his librettist was Morell; the oratorio was *Jephtha*.

OLD AGE AND INFIRMITY

*J*ephtha proved a real struggle to write. Halfway through the last chorus of Act II – whose text poignantly includes the words 'How dark O Lord are thy decrees, all hid from mortal sight' – Handel noted in the margin of his manuscript that he reached that point on 13 February but was unable to continue 'owing to a relaxation of the sight of my left eye'. Immediately after directing *Belshazzar,* he manfully recommenced his labours on his sixty-sixth birthday, 23 February. He finished the act but had to stop. Act III was begun in the middle of June and on 30 August the oratorio was at last finished. In the meantime, he had lost the sight of his left eye entirely, though he continued to play the organ as brilliantly as before. After directing the traditional performances of *Messiah* – now two of them, on 18 April and 16 May – at the Foundling Hospital he went with John Christopher Smith to Bath to take curative waters, but his eyesight got no better. Samuel Sharp of Guy's Hospital was able only to diagnose *gutta serena,* a term then generally used for a blindness that was without any other apparent symptoms of disease.

The sight in his right eye was also beginning to decline, but nevertheless Handel was able to conduct the première of *Jephtha* at Covent Garden on 26 February 1752, when the singers included Galli, Frasi and Beard. Mrs Delany thought it fine but very different from any other of Handel's oratorios when she heard it in 1756; Morell approved of it as his own favourite. Certainly, it includes some of Handel's deepest music, though it also borrows extravagantly, particularly from a collection of masses by the German composer Franz Habermann. The season also included performances of *Joshua* (14 and 19 February), *Hercules* (21 February), *Samson* (3 performances from 6

March), *Judas Maccabaeus* (18 and 20 March) and *Messiah* (25 and 26 March). As usual, the Foundling Hospital benefit performance of *Messiah* took place, this time early, on 9 April. But the condition of Handel's eyes continued to deteriorate. The *General Advertiser* reported in August 1752 that a 'Paralytick Disorder in his Head' had deprived him of sight entirely. There was to be no more composing of great significance.

John Christopher Smith the younger

The following November Handel underwent an operation, performed by William Bromfield, which involved the piercing of his cornea with a hooked needle and the depressing of the fluid beneath the pupil. The treatment was temporarily effective, enabling the composer to go outdoors, but by 27 January 1753 he was once more totally blind. The 1753 Lenten season got under way with him supervising but no longer in direct control of the performance of the music. The season included *Alexander's Feast* and *The Choice of Hercules* (9 March), *Jephtha* (16 and 21 March), *Judas Maccabaeus* (23 March and twice subsequently), *Samson* (4 April and twice subsequently) and, on 13 April, *Messiah*.

In the Foundling Hospital performance of *Messiah* on 1 May, Handel managed to play an organ concerto and a voluntary.

Unsurprisingly, his state of mind was not at this time a happy one. In March Lady Shaftsbury wrote in a letter of seeing him at the theatre 'dejected, wan, and dark'. She found an audience 'so insipid and tasteles (I may add unkind)' that they rewarded him with no applause. Handel nevertheless continued to impress with his brilliance on the organ at these occasions, though Burney notes that in the solo sections of his organ concertos he would often improvise rather than follow a printed score.

Handel continued to supervise the Lenten oratorio seasons, and new music still appeared each year. Burney asserts that Smith took most of it down from Handel's dictation. The Handel expert Anthony Hicks, however, has discovered that much of this 'new' material was either adapted from older music, some of it now lost, or redeployed directly. When,

A later portrait of Handel by Thomas Hudson, 1756

in 1757–8 Covent Garden presented an oratorio, *The Triumph of Time and Truth,* it was described as 'Altered from the Italian, with several new Additions'. In fact this was version number three of *Il trionfo del Tempo e del Disinganno* (1707), which Handel had substantially revised as *Il trionfo del Tempo e della Verità* in 1737. Morell provided a new English text, but the music itself was actually little changed from 1737, and Hicks suspects Smith's benevolent hand did most of the work involved. Late in 1757 there were also ostensibly new songs for Cassandra Frederick, a soprano who had played the harpsichord to Handel when she had been only eight years old. But these also come from old material, while the style of their refashioning suggests a more awkward hand than that of the grand old man.

As Handel's level of activity declined, so do detailed reports of his life and performances of his works. In 1754 the Lenten season opened with *Alexander Balus* on 1 March and continued with *Deborah* (13 March), *Saul* (17 March), *Joshua* (22 March), *Judas Maccabaeus* (27 March), *Samson* (29 March) and *Messiah* (1 April). On 15 April the Foundling Hospital performance of *Messiah* was given probably for the last time under Handel's direct supervision. Afterwards John Christopher Smith was appointed organist of the Hospital chapel, replacing Handel who 'excused himself from giving any further Instructions relating to the Performances' because of his health. On 12 March the Opera at the King's Theatre staged a revival of a revised version of *Admeto,* which Handel had written in 1727. It is a sobering thought to realize that this was the last performance of any Handel opera to have been attempted before our own century.

One more attempt at restoring Handel's sight might well have been made by the itinerant charlatan John Taylor, who also claimed to have treated J. S. Bach, fictitiously saying he was eighty-eight at the time (he died aged sixty-five) and had taught Handel (they never met). Bach also went totally blind, so any cure was conspicuously ineffectual. Taylor and Handel were both in Tunbridge Wells in August 1758, but apart from that fact no hard evidence exists that Handel submitted himself to the rogue's so-called medicine.

Handel's general health began a steady decline from now on. After the Covent Garden *Messiah* on 6 April 1759 he intended to set out for Bath to take the waters, but was not well enough to make the journey. He made a fourth codicil to his will, after having already adjusted it so that the Covent Garden organ would be left to John Rich and already deceased members of his own family would not be left irrelevant legacies. His final bequests were for the sum of £1,000 to go to the Society for the Support of Decayed Musicians and their Families, for various amounts of money to go to various friends, and, touchingly, for a year's extra wages to go to each of his servants. On Saturday 14 April, at eight o'clock in the morning, he died.

The last page of Handel's will, 1 June 1750

Handel in his last years, by an unknown hand

Despite his requests for a private burial in Westminster Abbey at least 3,000 people attended his funeral there on 20 April. He was buried in the South Cross, where, just over a century later, room was found (as Handel's undertaker insensitively pointed out it could be) to cram in another body in a grave immediately adjacent. (The space was eventually filled by the corpse of Charles Dickens.) Croft's *Burial Service* was sung by the combined Chapel Royal, St Paul's and Abbey Choirs. Three years later, Roubiliac's famous memorial was unveiled, the date of Handel's birth inscribed a year too early.

Handel's Development Of Style And Form

How did Handel develop the forms in which he worked? After all, apart from English oratorio, his single formal innovation, he concerned himself only with already established forms. What follows sums up very briefly his achievement in each of the fields he cultivated.

KEYBOARD MUSIC

Handel's keyboard music shows the same variety in planning as his other music, but individual movements cannot lay claim to being revolutionary or even particularly evolutionary. There are found the usual range of dances that feature in the now established baroque format of the *sonata da camera* (chamber sonata), as well as fugues, chaconnes and sets of variations. (The most famous of these variations are those known as 'The Harmonious Blacksmith', a movement that comes at the end of the E major Suite, published in 1720.) Yet although some of the music is unevenly finished – scholarly consensus has it that most of it dates from before 1720 – there is plenty to commend in the variety of invention. Room is found for improvisation, and Handel is far less strict than, say, Bach in maintaining rigidly a number of real parts, so already there is an unusual sense of freedom.

Most of the keyboard music was probably intended for domestic rather than public use, and some was used for the instruction of Handel's pupils. Some of it may come from as early as Handel's Hamburg years, though a quantity was written at Cannons. As usual, many ideas reappear in Handel's other works.

Arcangelo Corelli, the Italian composer and violinist who influenced Handel in Rome

CHAMBER MUSIC

While in Rome, Handel had come under the influence of Corelli, whose trio sonatas, all published in the last years of the eighteenth century, he must have got to know well. The trio sonatas of Handel's own Op. 2 set are in the form of the *sonata da chiesa* – two pairs of slow-fast movements, ostensibly not dances. The solo sonatas of Op. 1, like Op 2, published by Walsh in 1730, and the trios of Op. 5, published in 1739, are by contrast often in the more expansive (as far as number of movements is concerned), flexible and overtly secular *da camera* format. All are accomplished pieces, as are those examples Walsh did not publish (see work list). Freshly inventive and full of personal touches, they nevertheless break no new ground, simply serving to consolidate what Corelli achieved with the form.

ORCHESTRAL MUSIC

As we have seen, by far the greater part of Handel's orchestral music came about as a product of his innovation of inserting for variety's sake a concerto or two in the middle of his theatrical works. The major exceptions to this rule, the *Water Music* and the extravagantly scored *Music for the Royal Fireworks,* represent Handel at his ceremonial best.

Hidden in the canon there are a number of fairly early orchestral works. The overtures to *Il pastor fido, Teseo, Silla* and *Ottone* are thought to date from Handel's time in Hanover, for instance, just before he settled in England, while all three oboe concertos also come from around this time. The same probably applies to the six Op. 3 Concertos, even though they remained unpublished until 1734. Even so, these pieces include many marks of the typical Handel – vividly characterized ideas, strong contrapuntal working, and above all, unexpected colours and textures.

But for innovation, freedom and variety of texture, Handel never surpassed the twelve Grand Concertos, published as Op. 6, even though their original scoring admits no instruments outside the string family. (Handel added optional oboe parts to four concertos, but not very significant ones.) So radical was their impact at the time that Hawkins haughtily dismissed them as 'destitute of art and contrivance'. Obviously, like many critics then and now (I claim no dispensation), he was unable to see the wood for the trees. The dominant flavour of these hugely varied pieces is perhaps one of an improvisatory quality. The emotions in the set range wide, and Handel's only rule seems to be that rules are only a rough guide. The effect is like the best high baroque architecture, richly decorated to the point of anarchy yet still bound together by the

A copperplate engraving which accompanied the publication of the Water Music

very rules it threatens. A thrilling tension is created by the interplay between imagination and discipline.

The three *Concerti a due cori* of 1747–8 form a special group. Two of them Handel based on material used for earlier oratorios; all were played in Handel's latest oratorios at the time, and all reflect a flavour of magnificence and celebration not far removed from the world of the fireworks music. Just as these hybrids, scored for two wind groups and string *ripieno,* represented an extension of the concerto principle unique to Handel at the time, so did the genre of organ concerto, which Handel invented expressly for insertion into his oratorios. There are three distinct sets of these. The first, published by Walsh as Op. 4, comes from 1735–6; the second, which appeared in 1740 without opus number, includes two original compositions from 1739 and four arrangements from the Op. 6 Grand Concertos; and the third, unpublished until 1761, when it was numbered Op. 7, consists of works that date from between 1740 and 1751. Handel played these works himself, all except Op. 7 No. 1 on small instruments without pedals. While they do not possess the polish of the Op. 6 Concertos they are equally unpredictable in character and format. Indeed, the scores are full of *ad libitum* markings, occasionally applied to entire movements. One can only guess at the brilliance with which the composer improvised such passages in his own performances, but his standing as a keyboard virtuoso would suggest that it was something special.

SACRED MUSIC

O f Handel's church music only the *Brockes Passion* and a couple of motets seem not to have been designed for specific use. The occasions for which he composed other works in this category included private ceremonies in the chapel at Cannons (the Chandos Anthems) or at the Foundling Hospital, and ceremonial state services, such as those celebrating the Treaty of Utrecht (1713), the Coronation of George II (1727), the royal weddings of 1734 and 1736, Queen Caroline's funeral in 1737, the victory at Dettingen (1743) and the Peace of Aix-la-Chapelle (1748). In such works, his face is assuredly and appropriately a public one, except in the case of Queen Caroline's deeply personal funeral anthem. No composer since Purcell had risen to such challenges with such magnificent and uplifting music. Probably no composer since has managed to respond to such commissions without at least some measure of artistic compromise. Handel did not need to exercise that particular option. These events may have been a different kind of theatre from that to which he was accustomed, but theatre they were, and his responses to their particular dramas were as sure as ever.

An engraving of a contemporary chamber concert

SECULAR VOCAL CHAMBER MUSIC

The secular vocal music which Handel composed that does not broadly fit into the genres of opera and oratorio consists of the hundred or so cantatas written quickly to order, mostly in Italy, a generous score of duets and a couple of trios. The last seven duets were composed in London as late as 1741–5. Why he returned to the form then is a mystery, though as explained above they might have been calling-cards in preparation for a planned return to the European mainland. As also explained above, these seven duets are the sources of several choruses in *Messiah* and *Belshazzar*. Around twelve duets were copied in Hanover in or about 1711, and were probably composed there. They show the direct influence of the Italian composer Agostino Steffani. The remaining few come, like the cantatas, from Handel's period in Italy.

While they are of considerable value in themselves as miniature dramas designed for domestic performance in aristocratic salons, many of the cantatas can also be seen as important proving pieces, exploring with great freshness the subtleties of character and mood that distinguish Handel's operas. Indeed, sometimes the same music can be found in a cantata as in a scene from a later opera, sometimes heavily modified, sometimes not, but always translating effectively to the more exposed public arena.

OPERA

A s we have seen, *opera seria,* the form in which the younger Handel chose eventually to immerse himself, was a more or less fixed formula even in his hands: *da capo* aria (in the form A-B-A), recitative, the odd duet, a happy end. But though not an out-and-out reformist as Gluck was to be, Handel did loosen a few boundaries. Certain things were expected in *opera seria;* Handel's trick was to keep his audience guessing at whether those expectations would be met or not. In the apparently immovable ABA form of the *da capo* aria, for instance, he played with the introductory and concluding instrumental *ritornellos,* varying length and texture and even occurrence, matching the words' changing moods with corresponding changes of musical inflection. Nothing could be assumed, and the contrasts he introduced even within single arias were sometimes extraordinarily extreme.

Then there was his steady development of first the scene, then the act, then the entire opera, as a carefully layered entity which revealed and developed characters, relationships and dramatic situations through canny placement of arias and the use of such devices as strategic contrasts of key, orchestral colour, tempo, mode (major, minor) or language (openly diatonic, emotionally chromatic). Sometimes he associated particular characters with particular keys, and often a sudden change either in mood or in scene was marked by an equally sudden change in tonality.

His approach to recitative equally bore the marks of sophistication. The accompanied variety, used at dramatically crucial moments, is often as affecting as anything in Mozart, while his fluent mixture of different musical types – unaccompanied and accompanied recitative, arioso, fully fledged aria – in such episodes as Bajazet's suicide in *Tamerlano* or the depiction of the principal character's madness in *Orlando,* can be masterly. He even compromises the self-containment of the aria. In *Poro*, for instance, two estranged lovers interrupt each other's arias and in so doing create a highly effective, ironic and beautiful duet. Other devices, like the arioso-recitative-aria sequence where the aria, preceding an exit, discharges emotions and tensions built up by the arioso and recitative, or the incorporation of the closing chorus as part of an integrated sequence of climactic, thematically related numbers, anticipate later developments in Romantic opera. Neither was Handel always content with the conventional happy ending, though his eclecticism was such that in his later operas – *Ariodante, Alcina,* the third version of *Il pastor fido* – he was happy to incorporate elements of the French *opéra-ballet* – dancing and a separate chorus as opposed to the usual *mélange* of all the surviving *dramatis personae.*

Handel's operas come in three main varieties. First there is the conventionally heroic *opera seria,* in which the story usually comes from classical mythology or history and the subject is power and rivalry in both politics and love. Handel set three librettos by Metastasio in this mould – *Siroe, Poro* and *Ezio.* But this was a poet whose characterizations were limited by his dogged adherence to formal protocol, and the non-Metastasian heroic operas from 1724–5, *Giulio Cesare, Tamerlano* and *Rodelinda*, masterpieces all, show more fluidity, more credible a reflection of what human beings are really like and how they really feel.

The second category is the 'magic' opera, of which *Orlando* and *Alcina* are the outstanding representatives, though the other three, *Rinaldo, Teseo* and *Amadigi,* are scarcely failures musically or dramatically. In this genre, Handel allowed himself free flight of musical fantasy. Always adept at creating transformations of mood in music, the illogical and mystical elements of these plots appealed to him greatly.

Handel in his fifty-sixth year,
a copperplate engraving by E. N. Rollfsen from the
title page of Mattheson's biography of the composer

But it is in the third category, where there is a complex mixture of elements, including comedy, farce and parody as well as more serious things, that he is at perhaps his most sophisticated. In such works – *Serse, Agrippina, Flavio* and *Partenope* among them – he shows his profound understanding of human frailties and strengths. But it should be stressed that elements of the absurd and comic occur also in some of his most serious operas. He is able to see all sides of a dramatic situation. Above all, he writes music about people at their best and worst in a spirit of gentle understanding and sympathy.

ENGLISH ORATORIO

Circumstances conspired to make English oratorio, Handel's only genuinely radical innovation, his crowning achievement. For that we have the Bishop of London's anti-theatrical stance in the 1730s to thank, as well as the middle-class public's taste for being entertained in a grand manner while being morally improved and edified. The new form was, in any case, economically convenient. No expenses needed to be spent on staging, and because the involvement of the chorus was as critical as that of the soloists, and the soloists sang in English, money could also be saved by not employing the highest paid Italian virtuosi.

Handel, as one might expect, imported much from his experience of opera into the new form. All the dramatically effective devices written about in the preceding section came into play, but now rules could be even more relaxed. The fluidity the new form allowed him was something he exploited with relish. Since nobody had an exit, it was possible to dispense with the convention of the *da capo* aria whenever the situation demanded. Often in even his earliest oratorios – *Athalia* and *Saul,* for instance – Handel leads the ear to expect a *da capo* but suddenly breaks off and leads into something else. Compound forms, linking chorus and aria, were created, and intervening instrumental *sinfonie,* conveniently atmosphere-creating, replaced scene changes. Moreover, without visual illustration, aural suggestion could be taken to extremes. What the eyes beheld no longer placed limits on what the mind could imagine.

Thus, despite no requirement for staging – a condition often negated by performances earlier in our own century – the oratorios are authentic music-dramas.

The chorus generally represents the Israelites and also, sometimes, their opponents. Occasionally, it makes moralizing comment. But on the level of the individual, the plots are about the same interreactions of human strengths and weaknesses with which the operas concern themselves. Power struggles, jealousy and envy, the choices between principle and survival or position, tolerance or intolerance, magnanimity or cruelty, sanity or madness, love or hatred; and of course the bottom line, awareness of mortality. Just as in the operas, Handel writes with deep sympathy for the characters and the situations in which they find or wilfully put themselves. But there is a difference. In the oratorios the fate of individuals affects whole nations, so that everything that happens has consequences on two levels. And the music is the more telling because Handel does not often work with simplistic polarities. No person or nation is whiter than snow or blacker than coal. Even where right is palpably on one side, a people is just a people, guiltless of the political machinations of their leaders. Not, as *Athalia, Samson, Alexander Balus* and *Theodora* all show, that that precludes depicting the character of nations with suitably well-defined music.

A number of works stand out as different from the rest of the oratorios. Both *Messiah* and *Israel in Egypt* use texts taken exclusively from the Bible. They have no dramatic plot as such, and are really affirmations of Handel's own faith. The paradox is that their consequent popularity lured the public, then as now, into believing them to be archetypes of Handelian oratorio, which they are not. The greatness of *Messiah* lies not just in its level of inspiration but also in its fusion of the three great musical traditions of the time: Italian opera, German Passion and English anthem. *Israel in Egypt* cannot compare. This writer is not the only one who finds himself uncomfortable with its disproportionate use of the chorus and its consequent lack of a personal sensibility. Two other oratorios, *Semele* and *Hercules,* are also slightly different from the rest because they are classical dramas rather than biblical stories. *Semele* makes gods and heroes equally human, while *Hercules* has a powerfully dramatic force. These works have been called representatives of, respectively, the Homeric and Sophoclean sides of Handel.

Solomon and the highly individual *Susanna* are both vast if very different achievements, representing Handel's return to his most powerful after a relatively weak period, for which some of Morell's librettos and a number of weak plots had been at least partly responsible. And *Theodora,* with its tragi-heroic theme of martyrdom, and *Jephtha,* where the hero resigns himself to an equally tragic fate, crown a formidable output in music which again speaks of the human experience, with all its sorrows and joys, with profound understanding. Who is to say which of opera and oratorio represented Handel the better?

A miniature of the composer

Handel's Music In The Context Of The Age

HANDEL'S REPUTATION

Was Handel important in his own time? Certainly, at different times Handel's music held victorious sway in London, and it was also obviously a success abroad, as his well-documented visit to Dublin and widespread performances of his operas outside England testified. Some of his music, though no complete operas and oratorios save for *Alexander's Feast* and *Acis and Galatea,* was published in his own lifetime and presumably sold well. On such evidence, and on that provided by the newspapers, which seem to comment assiduously on his doings in London, he was unquestionably a celebrity for most of his time in England. Like all celebrities, he fell in and out of favour. Whether his music was important not as an isolated phenomenon but in the context of music in general is a different matter. Certainly he evolved a personal style and also a personal and flexible manner with even as naturally constrictive a form as *opera seria*. What is more, he invented a form – English oratorio – which remained more or less unique to him. Imitators like John Christopher Smith and John Stanley created pieces which were pale reflections of those of Handel, though Thomas Arne, with *Abel* (1744) and *Judith* (1764), did succeed in writing English oratorios in an individual style. Once Arne had died, however, the form went into hibernation until Mendelssohn and certain second-rate British composers rather clumsily resurrected it in a spirit of painful piety and pompousness in the next century.

But while Handel was undoubtedly the greatest practitioner of high baroque *opera seria,* he proved by his failure to gain a consistent following for it that the form was a dying breed, crying out for the reforms that composers such as Jomelli and Gluck (latterly influenced by the work of Rameau in France) brought to it. In a sense, Handel brought both genres, English oratorio and at least the baroque form of Italian *opera seria,* to full stops. Nothing more could be said by others without radical changes.

INFLUENCES ON HANDEL

H andel was naturally eclectic, even to the point of revolting against his own origins. His central reference point is really Italy; even in his Lutheran *Brockes Passion* there is little evidence of the influence of the most characteristic Germanic feature at that time, the chorale.

Significantly, Reinhard Keiser's music, which Handel got to know in Hamburg, shows some of the same Italian tendencies as Handel's – vivid orchestral colouring, strong accompanying rhythms. But Handel tends to make room for melodic breadth where Keiser does not, and that was a quality he honed to perfection in the crucial Roman years. By the time he got to England, Italian opera in Italy was beginning to change from being elaborately polyphonic to being predominantly homophonic, that is to say with tunes supported by simple, firm chordal progressions. That particular development entered Handel's language quite naturally, but unlike some others, he assimilated the new tendency without disgarding the old. Later came the influence of the English themselves, predominant among them Purcell, who offered Handel the best possible models for setting ceremonial English texts. Though he had died young, in 1695, Purcell's theatre music was still regularly played in London's theatres when Handel arrived. Something of his mannerisms of melody and, especially, harmony, can be traced in the younger composer's work in England, while in his later oratorios can be traced a directness of manner and an economy of utterance which fits the English language, with its Saxon monosyllables and terse structures, like a glove. In short, variety was the spice of Handel's music, and variety of texture especially. Grand and exotic, spare and intimate, all had a place, often in the same work. Balance of voice-types was crucial. It has been claimed that it is possible to detect for which particular singer a particular aria was written on the basis not only of its pitch range but of its style. Such sensitivity towards the character of his artists goes a long way towards explaining his penchant for revision.

Henry Purcell in a contemporary chalk drawing by Godfrey Kneller

But it is perhaps in his fascination with the unexpected that Handel's real originality lies. He liked to shock his listener, to turn rules upside-down, to throw in a phrase of unexpected length, to crash down on an unexpected chord, to explode in a sudden, magnificent *tutti* outburst, or curtly to take the volume down. In an age when the public could be casual about their listening, he forced audiences to lend their ears through the sheer strength of his imagination. But it was not all dramatic shock therapy. No composer was more adept at the typical baroque device of word-painting, as the evocation of the sun standing still in the oratorio *Joshua*, or the controversially realistic frogs and flies in *Israel in Egypt*, tell us. In all these respects, his sense of freedom and audacity resembles that of Haydn, or even Beethoven, whose wilful individuality and artistic self-determination he anticipates by three-quarters of a century. Always, but always, Handel's music speaks clearly and directly. He took what he wanted from those around him and those who came before him, digested it, added his own large personality and was simply, confidently but self-critically, and, despite many attempts at emulation, *inimitably* himself.

Handel's Music After His Death

Handel's Music After His Death

After Handel's death he was not forgotten. Oratorios concocted from his work poured forth from the hands of many others, eager to exploit his memory. Morell wrote new texts for several such *pasticii*, for instance *Nabal* (1764) and *Gideon*. Dr Samuel Arnold, official conductor of the Academy of Ancient Music and organist and composer to the Chapel Royal, 'adjusted' Handel's music and came up with *Omnipotence* and *Redemption*. Other *pasticii* included *Israel in Babylon* and *The Cure of Saul*. John Christopher Smith, no doubt drawing on the expertise gained from working with Handel in his last years, constructed *Paradise Lost, Rebecca* and *Nabal* itself. Though heretical, these exercises in opportunism did help Handel's status. He was the first composer ever to have a biography written about him, by Mainwaring. Moreover, this book included Robert Price's *Observations on the Works,* the first time one composer's output had been given some sort of coherent critical overview. But the age viewed Handel rather romantically, and not at all as a practical man of the theatre who made what he made through applying to his natural gifts sheer hard labour. Price and others saw his work as being flawed but with its flaws overcome by sublime visions. Others were naïvely uncritical. From our viewpoint, both factions seem wide of the mark.

Handel's music was valued partly because of the new fashion in the later eighteenth century for reclaiming 'ancient' music. Both the Academy of Ancient Music and the Concerts of Antient Music, for instance, regularly included his work in their programmes; indeed it seems to have dominated them. Then, in 1783, three patrons,

Sir Watkin Williams Wynn, the Earl of Sandwich and Joah Bates, the Earl's secretary, hatched the idea of mounting a vast commemoration the following year, mistakenly believing 1784 to be the centenary of Handel's birth. What they planned was a grand, overtly nationalistic festival to take place in Westminster Abbey and at the nearby Pantheon over three days in May, with *Messiah* as the climax. Vast forces were assembled – 513 performers in all. In the Abbey a combined organ and harpsichord console was installed from which Bates directed. The orchestra included six trombones, then a rarely found instrument in any orchestra, and a double bassoon, as well as a particularly large variety of kettle drum in addition to the set from the Tower which Handel had often used in his own performances. *The European Magazine* reported the occasion thus: 'The immense volume and torrent of sound was almost too much for the head or the senses to bear – we were elevated into a species of delirium . . . .'. Such was the success of the festival that the Abbey concerts were repeated, to equal acclaim.

Some resented Handel's enduring popularity. Burney was one, though being an employee of the King he could hardly openly express his preference for Neapolitan opera over Handel's *opera seria* until later. Others, like the poet William Cowper, regretted that *Messiah* seemed to have been given on this occasion for the greater glory of Handel and England rather than for that of God.

Nevertheless annual commemorations followed with ever expanding forces: 616 musicians took part in 1785, 640 in 1786, 806 in 1787. By 1791 numbers had increased to 1,068. Against such a background, in 1785 Samuel Arnold had begun his pioneering attempt to publish Handel's complete works, encouraged by King George III's advance order for twenty-five copies of each volume.

The 1791 Commemoration was the last of the eighteenth century. But the grandiose approach to Handel's music had already spread to other English centres. 'Monster' performances of *Messiah* were heard in York, Manchester, Birmingham and Sheffield. Burney's personal notebook betrays a private thought that he dared not utter publicly – that 'our reverence for old authors and bigotry to Handel . . . has prevented us from keeping pace with the rest of Europe in the cultivation of music'. It was quite true. Handel's music, and only a small selection from the massive *corpus* he left at that, now dominated concert and festival programming throughout the nation, not just at the Academy of Ancient Music and the Concerts of Antient Music.

Meanwhile, it had also travelled further afield. *Messiah* reached its first German public – appropriately in Hamburg – on 21 May 1772. The intellectual Johann Adam Hiller, an ardent champion, later re-orchestrated the work, as, famously, did Mozart for Vienna in 1789. Mozart also made arrangements of *Acis and Galatea*, the *St Cecilia Ode* and *Alexander's Feast*. In England, such transformations were rather

George III, a supporter of Arnold's attempt to publish Handel's complete works

frowned upon; gargantuan the size of English orchestras and choirs may have been, but at least they respected more strictly than Mozart the original distribution of parts. Haydn, having heard the 1791 commemoration performance, later took back to Vienna the libretto for his own masterpiece and tribute to Handel's achievement, *The Creation.* Beethoven also revered him above all composers, and was filled with joy when he was given the Arnold edition by Johannn Stumff near the end of his life.

In the early years of the nineteenth century English musical festivals continued to be obsessed with Handel's music, and in 1834 the Handel Commemorations resumed in Westminster Abbey. There may have been a mere 644 musicians that year, but the effect was still overwhelming according to observers, who included the future Queen Victoria. Vincent Novello was the organist. Soon, in 1844, his family's company was to take over the fledgling *Musical Times,* a publication whose aim was to provide amateur choral societies with music cheaply. In 1846 Vincent Novello's vocal score of *Messiah* was published, followed by *Judas Maccabaeus* and Haydn's *Creation.* Half-price editions of the choruses only were made available. The experiment was a vast success and largely responsible for bringing Handel's work, for so long the province of the privileged, to the masses. Oratorio had become immensely popular, though listening to it was regarded more as a moral exercise than anything, almost like going to church.

As in England, to lesser degree also in Germany, though France was more circumspect; indeed Berlioz was thoroughly rude about Handel. Not until 1873 was *Messiah* given a complete performance in Paris, though by 1900 it had achieved such status that it was chosen for performance at the opening of the Paris Exposition. By contrast, the United States quickly took Handel to heart almost as soon as visitors arrived from Dublin in 1770 with excerpts from *Messiah.* Extracts from both this work, and others from Handel's popular oratorios, became commonplace features of American

The original score for Judas Maccabaeus

concert programmes. Manuscript copies of *Messiah,* dating from 1780 and 1790 (the latter in Mozart's version) still survive in Pennsylvania, though it was not until 1818 that the work was heard complete, in Boston under the auspices of the Handel and Haydn Society.

Enthusiasm in England for Handel's oratorios continued unabated throughout the latter half of the nineteenth century. In 1857 a 'Festival of the People in honour of Handel' was held in the great Crystal Palace that had recently been moved to South London from Hyde Park. 2,000 singers and 500 instrumentalists were reported to have taken part, though the accoustics were not conducive to clarity. Two years later, a repeat performance was given under better conditions, the hall now equipped with a false roof and accoustic baffles. Now there were even more performers: 2,765 singers and an orchestra of 460. The festival was established as a triennial event, though there was a special festival in 1885 to commemorate the bicentenary of Handel's birth. If numbers of performers were vast, audience figures were commensurately astronomical. In the 1883 commemoration, 4,000 sang, 500 played and in all 87,769 heard.

Performances with such figures, of course, had little to do with any realistic vision of what Handel's music was all about. They were rallies, occasions when national pride, even above the religious fervour whose flames the grand performances of the previous century had been designed to fan, would be swollen to what we in post-colonial times would see – should see – as a tasteless degree.

Despite early criticism to that effect by some – George Bernard Shaw wrote that he would 'propose a law making it a capital offence to perform an oratorio by Handel with more than eighty performers' – the vast Crystal Palace performances continued for a long time. The last one took place in 1926, with Britain ironically in the midst of economic despair and the General Strike. Yet there was already a trend to negate this heinous, wholesale inflation and distortion of Handel's music. The pioneering scholar-performer Arnold Dolmetsch published and performed some chamber works in the 1890s; the young Adrian Boult conducted a sane edition by Julian Herbage of *Acis and Galatea* with reasonably modest forces for the BBC. Then unfamiliar oratorios began to be unearthed, among them *Semele,* though often they were presented as if operas, with all the cumbersome movements of chorus that meant.

While the real operas, with one or two exceptions, continued to be ignored in England, Germany boldly took some of them on, starting with *Rodelinda* in Göttingen in 1920. Astonishingly, this was the first performance of any Handel opera anywhere since 1754. Halle, Münster, Berlin and Leipzig all staged operas by Handel in the subsequent decade, though the style, in reaction to Wagnerian naturalism, tended to be abstract and experimental. Oskar Hagen, an art historian, was the man largely responsible for this renaissance, though he respected neither the dramatic fluidity nor the written note to any great degree. In fact, his productions consciously aimed to be static, while, for instance, high castrato parts would as a matter of course be transposed down an octave, and the treatment meted out to the recitative could perhaps best be described as liberal.

After the Nazi's absurd wartime attempts to 'Aryanize' Handel – *Judas Maccabaeus* became *William of Nassau, Israel in Egypt* would become *Mongolensturm (Mongol Fury)* – German performances of Handel's operas in the immediate postwar period tended to continue in Hagen's free, abstract vein. Meanwhile, the formation of the pioneering Handel Opera Society in 1955 gave the green light for resuscitation on British stages. Progress was slow, but the rise of internationalism and of period-style performance practice as a central part of European and American musical culture in the eighties and nineties, together with the recording industry's conversion to that cause and the development of a huge market for the medium of the compact disc, has helped Handel's cause, both operatic and otherwise, tremendously. Our own generation has the privilege to see perhaps for the first time Handel's great legacy in a clear light.

A Note On Performing Styles

Any musician contemplating a performance of a large-scale work by Handel first has to answer two questions: what and how? The first of these questions might seem superfluous. You surely and simply take a creditable edition of the work concerned and perform the music it contains. But there is more to it than that. John Walsh published only two dramatic works in Handel's own lifetime, *Alexander's Feast* in 1738 and *Acis and Galatea* in 1743. The other oratorios he issued sporadically only after Handel's death. Later in the eighteenth century, Samuel Arnold began a proposed complete edition, the first time such an enterprise had been undertaken for any composer. Between 1787 and 1790, much to Arnold's credit, 180 parts appeared in print. But only five of the Italian operas were included, and the musical text itself was far from reliable. The English Handel Society, founded in 1843, was the next organization seriously to tackle the problem of giving Handel his due, but the sixteen volumes which appeared, containing selected oratorios, anthems and duets, hardly improved on what Arnold had accomplished. Friedrich Chrysander, under the auspices of the Handel-Gesellschaft, edited, almost on his own, ninety-three volumes between 1858 and 1903, using a collection of performance material in Hamburg in preference to the autographs which were also available to him. Even the latest effort, the Hallische Händel-Ausgabe, began its life in 1958 using the kind of scholarly principles that meant it was still some way from being the fully critical edition it now aims to be.

The consequences of all this are many. First, there is still the problem that a work might not be available in any credible version at all. The Hallische Händel-Ausgabe is still far from complete. Second, it is often impossible for a performer to be sure that what he is reading in print really represents Handel's intentions at any one time, given the hotch-potch way in which material has often been assembled for printing. We know that Handel was constantly revising his theatrical works for stage performance. Even so, the idea that a modern interpretation should in any case slavishly follow an order of service sanctioned at one time or another by the composer is surely outdated. While it is often important to preserve the overall balance in the structure of a particular scene, that structure is not necessarily harmed by supposedly inauthentic substitutions. If we know that Handel chose substitution A and substitution B in one performance and substitution C and substitution D in another, is there any reason for a conductor not to choose substitution A with substitution D just because Handel himself never used that particular combination? Conductors should surely be permitted the exercise of such freedom in harness with sensitivity and reason.

The same argument applies to style of interpretation. While it has become commonplace in recent times for period-style orchestras to play baroque music – and there are countless arguments in favour, such as the well-defined timbres the practice induces – orchestras of conventional modern instruments can nevertheless be encouraged to learn and apply lessons from their period-style counterparts. All musicians have ears and brains. Admittedly, it is still difficult to get an orchestra to 'unlearn' nineteenth century mannerisms, but it need not be impossible. As for numbers of performers, we can to a certain extent follow known examples. But theatres in Handel's day were different in size and acoustics from most theatres today. The only maxim should be that what works in any given circumstance must have right on its side. We have to approximate in any case with singers, because debate still rages

*Handel's monument in the Marktplatz,
Halle, erected in 1859 by Hermann Heidel*

furiously over how they sounded in the eighteenth century. We know that sopranos were considered to be in their prime at a far younger age than today; castratos no longer exist at all and countertenors, though getting stronger and higher by the year, are no surefire substitute for them. Even the boys of the choirs who sang in that pioneering performance under Bernard Gates of the oratorio *Esther* in the Crown and Anchor Tavern in 1732 must have sounded different from the best choirboys today, since voices broke much later in life then. So in attempting to regain the spirit of that age – which, we must remember, is also to reflect the spirit of our own age – we can only make guesses, unwittingly exercising our prejudices, whatever they may be. Who knows, in a hundred years fashion may have turned full circle and we will again be advocating the monster performances of *Messiah* that started with the 1784 Handel Commemoration Festival. Already, Mozart's wonderful versions of *Messiah*, *Acis und Galatea* (as Mozart called it) and other works have been rehabilitated not as heretical aberrations but as valid views from a later age.

The majority of Handel's works are not numbered. The following
list is ordered, where possible, according to the dates of the works;
entries whose dates are not known begin the list. Some of the works
ascribed to Handel are now thought to be of doubtful authorship
and they are not included.

Alceste

Alleluia . . . amen, D minor

Alleluia . . . amen, D minor

Alleluia . . . amen, G major

Alleluia . . . amen, A minor

Alleluia . . . amen, F major

Alleluia . . . amen, F major

Amen, F major

Amen . . . alleluia, G minor

Anthem, Te decus virginem

Aria [hornpipe], C minor

2 Arias, F major

Cantata, Ah, che pur troppo è vero

Cantata, Ah che troppo ineguali

Cantata, Allor ch'io dissi

Cantata, Alpestre monte

Cantata, Bella ma ritrosetta

Cantata, Care selve

Cantata, Chi ben ama

Cantata, Clori degli occhi miei

Cantata, Clori, mia bella Clori

Cantata, Clori ove sei

Cantata, Cuopre tal volta

Cantata, Dal fatale momento

Cantata, Dimmi, o mio cor

Cantata, Dolce pur d'amor l'affanno

Cantata, E partirai, mia vita?

Cantata, Figli del mesto cor

Cantata, Figlio d'alte speranze

Cantata, Fra pensieri quel pensiero

Cantata, Irene, idolo mio

Cantata, Mi palpita il cor

Cantata, Nel dolce dell'oblio (Pensieri notturni di Filli)

Cantata, Nel dolce tempo

Cantata, Nell' africane selve

Cantata, Nice che fa? che pensa?

Cantata, Non sospirar, non piangere

Cantata, Occhi miei, che faceste?

Cantata, O lucenti, o sereni occhi

Cantata, Parti, l'idolo mio

Cantata, Qualor crudele si mia vaga Dori

Cantata, Qual sento io non conosciuto

Cantata, Sans y penser

Cantata, Sarai contenta un di

Cantata, Siete rose rugiadose

Cantata, S'il ne falloit (Cantate françoise)

Cantata, Solitudini care, amata libertà

Cantata, Spande ancor

Cantata, Splende l'alba in oriente

Cantata, Stelle, perfide stelle (Partenza di G. B.)

Cantata, Torna il core al suo diletto

Cantata, Tra le fiamme

Cantata, Un sospir a chi si muove

Cantata, Vedendo amor

Cantata, Venne voglia ad amore

Coro and [Bourrée], B♭ major

Duet, A miravi io son intento

Duet, Quel fior ch'all'alba nasce

Duo, F major

Gavotte, G minor

Gigue, B♭ major

Hymn, O love divine, how sweet thou art (Desiring to Love)

Hymn, Rejoice, the Lord is King (On the Resurrection)

Hymn, Sinners obey the Gospel word (The Invitation)

Jubilate, 'Chandos', D major

March, G major

Minuet and Coro, B♭ major

Organ concerto, A major

Rigadon and Bourrée, G minor

Sarabande, F major

Sinfonia, B♭ major

Solo sonatas with bassoon (12 published as Opus 1) (c. 1730):
No. 1, recorder, A minor
No. 2, recorder, B♭ major
No. 3, recorder, C major
No. 4, recorder, D minor
No. 5, recorder, F major
No. 6, recorder, G minor
No. 7, flute, E minor
No. 8, oboe, B♭ major
No. 9, oboe, C minor
No. 10, ?oboe, F major
No. 11, violin, A major
No. 12, violin, D major
No. 13, violin, D minor
No. 14, violin, G major
No. 15, violin, G minor
No. 16, viola da gamba, G minor
No. 17, violin, A major

2 songs:
Sans y penser, chanson
Quand on suit l'amoureuse loix, chanson

3 songs:
Ein hoher Geist muss immer höher denken
Endlich muss man doch entdecken
In deinem schönen Mund

6 songs:
Son d'Egitto
Aure, più non bacciate
Porta la braccia al seno
Gran guerrier di tua virtù
Quanto dolci, quanto cari
Non posso dir di più

Song, As Celia's fatal arrows (The Unhappy Lovers)

Song, As on a sunshine summer's day

Song, Ask not the cause (Charming Chloris)

Song, Bacchus one day gaily striding
(Bacchus' Speech in Praise of Wine)

Song, Der Mund spricht zwar gezwungen Nein (Air en
lange allemand)

Song, Dizente mis oyos (Air en lange espagnole)

The morning is charming (Hunting Song)

Song, Oh! cruel tyrant love (Strephon's Complaint of Love)

Song, On the shore of a low-ebbing sea
(The Satyr's Advice to a Stock Jobber)

Song, Says my uncle, I pray you discover
(Molly Mog, or The Fair Maid of the Inn)

Trio sonata, No. 14, C minor

Trio sonata, No. 15, F major

Trio sonata, No. 16, G minor

Trio sonata, No. 17, E major

Trio sonata, No. 18, E minor

Trio sonata, No. 19, F major

Trio sonata, No. 20, C major

Oboe concerto No. 3, G minor (?1703)

Almira (1705)

Nero (1705)

Laudate pueri Dominum, F major (1706)

7 items (1707):
Sans y penser, chanson
S'il ne falloit
Petite fleur brunette, air
Vous, qui m'aviez procuré
Nos plaisirs seront peu durabble, air
Vous ne sauriez flatter

Non, je ne puis plus souffrir, air

Cantata, Ah! crudel nel pianto mio (c. 1707)

Cantata, Alla caccia (Diana cacciatrice) (1707)

Cantata, Aure soavi e liete (1707)

Cantata, Cor fedele (Clori, Tirsi e Fileno) (1707)

Cantata, Da quel giorno fatale (Il delirio amoroso) (1707)

Cantata, Dietro l'orme fuggaci (Armida abbandonata) (1707)

Cantata, Donna che in ciel (1707)

Cantata, Menzognere speranze (1707)

Cantata, Nella stagion, che di viole (1707)

Cantata, Ne' tuoi lumi, o bella Clori (1707)

Cantata, Poichè giuraro amore (1707)

Cantata, Qualor l'egre pupille (1707)

Cantata, Sarei troppo felice (1707)

Cantata, Sei pur bella, pur vezzosa (La bianca rosa) (1707)

Cantata, Se per fatal destino (1707)

Cantata spagnuola, No se enmendará jamás (1707)

Cantata, Tu fedel? tu costante? (1707)

Cantata, Udite il mio consiglio (1707)

Cantata, Un alma innamorata (1707)

Coelestis dum spirat aura, D major/G major (1707)

Dixit Dominus, G minor (1707)

Duet, Caro autor di mia doglia (c,1707)

Duet, Giù nei tartarei regni (c. 1707–9)

Haec est regina virginum, anthem (1707)

Il trionfo del Tempo e del Disinganno (1707)

Laudate pueri Dominum, D major (1707)

Nisi Dominus, G major (1707)

O qualis de caelo sonus, G major (1707)

Overture, B♭ major (?1707)

Rodrigo (1707)

Saeviat tellus inter vigores, D major (1707)

Salve regina, G minor, anthem (1707)

Violin Concerto, B♭ major (c. 1707)

Cantata, Amarilli vezzosa (Il duello amoroso) (1708)

Cantata, Arresta il passo (Aminta e Fillide) (1708)

Cantata, Clori vezzosa Clori (1708)

Cantata, Dite, mie piante (1708)

Cantata, Dunque sarà pur vero (Agrippina condotta a morire) (1708)

Cantata, Hendel, non può mia musa (1708)

Cantata, La terra è liberata (Apollo e Dafne) (1708)

Cantata, Lungi da voi, che siete poli (1708)

Cantata, Lungi dal mio bel nume (1708)

Cantata, Lungi n'andò Fileno (1708)

Cantata, Manca pur quanto sai (1708)

Cantata, Mentre il tutto è in furore (1708)

Cantata, Notte placida e cheta (1708)

Cantata, O come chiare e belle (Olinto, Il Tebro, Gloria) (1708)

Cantata, Qual ti riveggio, oh Dio (1708)

Cantata, Quando sperasti, o core (1708)

Cantata, Se pari è la tua fe (1708)

Cantata, Sorge il di (Aci, Galatea e Polifemo) (1708)

Cantata, Stanco di più soffrire (1708)

Der beglückte Florindo; Die verwandelte Daphne (1708)

Duet, Se tu non lasci amore (1708)

Oratorio per la Resurrezione di Nostro Signor Gesù Cristo (1708)

Trio, Quel fior ch'all'alba ride (?c. 1708)

Agrippina (1709)

Cantata, Chi rapi la pace (1709)

Cantata, Dalla guerra amorosa (1709)

Cantata, Da sete ardente afflitto (1709)

Cantata, Del bel idolo mio (1709)

Cantata, Filli adorata e cara (1709)

Cantata, Fra tante pene (1709)

Cantata, Lungi da me pensier tiranno (1709)

Cantata, Ninfe e pastori (1709)

Cantata, O numi eterni (La Lucrezia) (1709)

Cantata, Sento là che ristretto (1709)

Cantata, Zeffiretto, arresta il volo (1709)

The Alchemist (1710)

[Cantata per Carlo VI] (1710)

Duet, Amor gioje mi porge (1710–1)

Duet, Che vai pensando (1710–1)

Duet, Conservate, raddoppiate (1710–1)

Duet, Quando in calma ride il mare (1710–1)

Duet, Sono liete, fortunate (1710–1)

Duet, Tacete, ohime, tacete (1710–1)

Duet, Tanti strali al sen (1710–1)

Duet, Troppo cruda (1710–1)

Duet, Va, speme infida (1710–1)

Anthem, As pants the hart, D minor (1711–4)

Cantata, Behold, where Venus weeping stands (Venus and Adonis) (171

Cantata, Giunta l'ora fatal (Il pianto di Maria) (1711)

Duet, Langue, geme e sospira (?1711)

Rinaldo (1711)

Trio, Se tu non lasci amore (?1711)

Il pastor fido (1712)

Anthem, O sing unto the Lord, G major (1712–4)

Jubilate, 'Utrecht', D major (1713)

Ode for the Birthday of Queen Anne (Eternal source of light divine) (?1713)

Silla (1713)

Te Deum, 'Utrecht', D major (1713)

Teseo (1713)

Te Deum, 'Caroline', D major (1714)

Amadigi di Gaula (1715)

Der für die Sünde der Welt gemartete und sterbende
Jesus [Brockes Passion] (1716)

Orchestral suite, F major (c. 1716–7)

'Chandos' anthem, As pants the hart, E minor (1717–8)

'Chandos' anthem, Have mercy upon me,
O God, C minor (1717–8)

'Chandos' anthem, In the Lord put I my trust,
D minor (1717–8)

'Chandos' anthem, I will magnify thee,
O God, A major (1717–8)

'Chandos' anthem, Let God arise, B♭ major (1717–8)

'Chandos' anthem, My song shall be alway, G major (1717–8)

'Chandos' anthem, O be Joyful ('Chandos' jubilate),
D major (1717–8)

'Chandos' anthem, O come let us sing unto the Lord,
A major (1717–8)

'Chandos' anthem, O praise the Lord with one consent,
E major (1717–8)

'Chandos' anthem, O sing unto the Lord
F major (1717–8)

'Chandos' anthem, The Lord is my light,
G minor (1717–8)

Sonata [concerto], G minor (c. 1717)

Water Music (1717):
Suite, F major
Suite, D major
Suite, G major

Acis and Galatea (1718)

Cantata, L'aure grate, il fresco rio (La solitudine) (1718)

Esther (1718)

Te Deum, 'Chandos', B♭ major (c. 1718)

Song, Di godere la speranza (c. 1719)

Song, Oh my dearest, my lovely creature (c. 1719)

Keyboard (probably before 1720 unless stated):

No. 1–4 Suite, A major (1720)
No. 5 Air, A major
No. 6 Allemande, A major
No. 7 Passepied, A major
No. 15 Prelude, A minor
No. 16 Allegro, A minor
No. 17 Fugue, A minor
No. 18 Prelude, A minor
No. 19 Lesson, A minor
No. 20 Sonatina, A minor
No. 21 Allemande, A minor
No. 25–26 Suite, B minor
No. 27 Fugue, B minor

No. 30–33 Suite, B♭ major

No. 34–36 Suite, B♭ major

No. 37 Fugue, B♭ major

No. 38 Air, B♭ major

No. 39 Air, B♭ major

No. 40 Sonatina, B♭ major

No. 50–54 Suite, C major

No. 55 Chaconne (with 49 variations), C major

No. 56–8 Sonata, C major

No. 59 Sonata, C major

No. 60 Fantasia, C major

No. 62 Air, C major

No. 63 Passepied, C major

No. 64 Prelude (Allegro), C major

No. 70–3 Suite, C minor

No. 74–8 Suite (Partita), C minor

No. 79–81 Suite, C minor

No. 82 Air, C minor

No. 83 Fugue, C minor

No. 90 March, D major

No. 91 Passepied, D major

No. 95–99 Suite, D minor

No. 100–6 Suite, D minor

No. 107–11 Suite, D minor

No. 112–7 Suite, D minor (new for 1720)

No. 118–22 Suite, D minor (1720s)

No. 123–6 Suite, D minor (1739)

No. 127 [Hornpipe], D minor

No. 128 Prelude, D minor

No. 129 Prelude, D minor

No. 130 Prelude, D minor

No. 131 Sonata (Allegro), D minor

No. 132 Sonatina, D minor

No. 145–8 Suite, E major (new for 1720)

No. 149 Prelude, E major

No. 150 Fugue, E major

No. 151 Sarabande/Minuet, E major

No. 160–2 Suite, E minor

No. 163–7 Suite, E minor

No. 175–9 Suite/Sonata, F major

No. 180 Air, F major

No. 181 Air (with 2 variations), F major

No. 182 Allemande, F major (c. 1730–5)

No. 183 Capriccio, F major

No. 184 Chaconne, F major

No. 185 Fugue, F major

No. 186 Gigue, F major

No. 187 Prelude, F major

No. 193–7 Suite, F minor

No. 198 Prelude, F minor

No. 204–7 Suite, F♯ minor

No. 208 Prelude, F♯ minor

No. 211–6 Suite (Partita), G major

No. 217–23 Suite, G major

No. 224–5 Prelude and Capriccio, G major

No. 226–7 Concerto, G major

No. 228 Chaconne (with 62 variations), G major

No. 229 Chaconne (with 20/21 variations), G major

No. 230 Chaconne/Aria (with 5 variations), G major

No. 231 Fugue, G major

No. 232 Sonata, G major

No. 233 Gavotte, G major

No. 234 Sonatina (Fuga), G major

No. 241–2 Overture, G minor

No. 243–5 Suite, G minor

No. 246–9 Suite, G minor

No. 250–5 Suite, G minor

No. 256–9 Suite, G minor

No. 260–3 Suite, G minor (1739)

No. 264 Fugue, G minor

No. 265–6 Prelude and allegro, G minor

No. 267 Air, G minor

No. 268 Air, G minor

No. 269 Bourée ('Impertinence'), G minor

No. 270 Capriccio, G minor (c. 1720)

No. 271 Chaconne, G minor

No. 272 Prelude, G minor

No. 273 Sonata, G minor

No. 274 Sonatina, G minor

No. 275 Sonatina, G minor (c. 1749–50)

No. 276 Toccata, G minor

No. 277–8 Suite, G minor

No. 279 Prelude on Jesu meine Freude, G minor

Anthem, As pants the hart, D minor (early 1720s)

Radamisto (1720)

Charming is your shape and air
(the Polish minuet, or Miss Kitty [The Reproof]) (1720)

Song, Cloe proves false (The Slighted Swain) (c. 1720)

Song, Ye winds to whom Collin compains
(An Answer to Collin's Complaint) (c. 1720)

Anthem, As pants the hart, D minor (1721–6)

Anthem, I will magnify Thee, O God, A major (1721–6)

Anthem, Let God arise, A major (1721–6)

Cantata, Crudel tiranno amor (1721)

Floridante (1721)

Muzio Scevola (1721)

Te deum, A major (1721–6)

Song, Faithless, ungrateful
(The Forsaken Maid's Complaint) (1722)

Overture, D major (c. 1722–3)

Trio sonata, No. 1, Opus 2, No. 1, B minor (1722–33)

Trio sonata, No. 2, Opus 2, No. 2, G minor (1722–33)

Trio sonata, No. 3, Opus 2, No. 3, B♭ major (1722–33)

Trio sonata, No. 4, Opus 2, No. 4, F major (1722–33)

Trio sonata, No. 5, Opus 2, No. 5, G minor (1722–33)

Trio sonata, No. 6, Opus 2, No. 6, G minor (1722–33)

Flavio, Rè di Longobardi (1723)

Ottone, Rè di Germania (1723)

9 arias (1724–7):
 Künft'ger Zeiten eitler Kummer
 Das zitternde Glänzen der spielenden Wellen
 Süsser Blumen Ambraflocken
 Süsse Stille, sanfter Quelle
 Singe, Seele, Gott zum Preise
 Meine seele hört im Sehen
 Die ihr aus dunklen Grüften
 In der angenehmen Büschen

Flammende Rose, Zierde der Erden

Giulio Cesare in Egitto (1724)

Tamerlano (1724)

Elpidia, arrangement (1725)

Rodelinda, Regina de' Longobardi (1725)

Song, The sun was sunk beneath the hill
(The Poor [Despairing] Shepherd) (c. 1725)

Song, 'Twas when the seas were roaring
(The Melancholy Nymph [The Faithful Maid]) (c.1725)

Song, When I survey Clarinda's charms
(Matchless Clarinda [The Rapture]) (c. 1725)

Song, Why will Florella when I gaze (Florella) (c. 1725)

Alessandro (1726)

Scipione (1726)

Admeto, Rè de Tessaglia (1727)

Cantata, Deh! lasciate e vita e volo (1727)

Cantata, [H]o fuggito amore (1727)

Cantata, Son gelsomino (Il gelsomino) (1727)

Coronation anthem, Let thy hand be strengthened, G major (1727)

Coronation anthem, My heart is inditing, D major (1727)

Coronation anthem, The king shall rejoice, D major (1727)

Coronation anthem, Zadok the Priest (1727)

Riccardo Primo, Rè d'Inghilterra (1727)

Song, È troppo bella, troppo amorosa (1727)

Siroe, Rè di Persia (1728)

Tolomeo, Rè di Egitto (1728)

Lotario (1729)

Minuets (1729)

Silete venti, B♭, major (1729)

Ormisda, arrangement (1730)

Partenope (1730)

Poro, Rè dell'Indie (1731)

Venceslao, arrangement (1731)

Catone, arrangement (1732)

Ezio (1732)

Lucio Papirio, arrangement (1732)

Sosarme, Rè di Media (1732)

Athalia (1733)

Caio Fabbricio, arrangement (1733)

Deborah (1733)

March, G major (1733)

March, G major (1733)

Orlando (1733)

Semiramide, arrangement (1733)

Water Piece, D major (1733)

Anthem, This is the day, D major (1734)

Arbace, arrangement (1734)

Arianna in Creta (1734)

Concerti Grossi, Opus 3 (1734):
No. 1, B♭ major
No. 2, B♭ major
No. 3, G major
No. 4, F major
No. 5, D minor
No. 6, D major/D minor

Il Parnasso in festa (1734)

Oreste (1734)

Overture, F major (c. 1734)

Song, Phillis be kind (1734)

Song, Venus now leaves her Paphian dwelling (1734)

Alcina (1735)

Ariodante (1735)

'Tunes for Clay's Musical Clock': F major, C major, C major,
C major, F major, C major, C major, G major, C major, C major,
C major (c. 1735–45)

Alexander's Feast (1736)

Anthem, Sing unto God, D major (1736)

Atalanta (1736)

Cantata, Cecilia, volgi un sguardo (1736)

Cantata, Languia di bocca lusinghiera
[Look down, harmonious saint] (?1736)

Didone, arrangement (1736)

Double violin and cello concerto, C major (1736)

Song, Not Cloe that I better am (1736)

Arminio (1737)

Berenice (1737)

Cantata, Carco sempre di gloria (1737)

Giustino (1737)

Il trionfo del Tempo e della Verità (1737)

Song, I like the amorous youth that's free (c. 1737)

Suite des pièces, F major (c. 1737–8)

The ways of Zion do mourn (Funeral anthem), G minor (1737)

Alessandro Severo (1738)

Faramondo (1738)

Organ concerto, D minor (?c. 1738)

Serse (1738)

Six organ concertos, Opus 4 (1738):
No. 1, G minor/G major
No. 2, B♭ major
No. 3, G minor

No. 4, F major
No. 5, F major
No. 6, B♭ major

Cantata, Qual fior che all'alba ride (1739)

Giove in Argo (1739)

Harpsichord concerto, G major (c. 1739)

Israel in Egypt (1739)

Ode for St. Cecilia's Day (1739)

Song, Phyllis the lovely, turn to your Swain
(Phillis Advised) (c. 1739)

Saul (1739)

Trio sonata, No. 7, Opus 5, No. 1, A major (1739)

Trio sonata, No. 8, Opus 5, No. 2, D major (1739)

Trio sonata, No. 9, Opus 5, No. 3, E minor (1739)

Trio sonata, No. 10, Opus 5, No. 4, G major (1739)

Trio sonata, No. 11, Opus 5, No. 5, G minor (1739)

Trio sonata, No. 12, Opus 5, No. 6, F major (1739)

Trio sonata, No. 13, Opus 5, No. 7, B♭ major (1739)

Twelve Grand Concertos in seven parts for strings, Opus 6 (1739):

No. 1, G major
No. 2, F major
No. 3, C minor
No. 4, A minor
No. 5, D major
No. 6, G minor
No. 7, B♭ major
No. 8, C minor
No. 9, F major
No. 10, D minor
No. 11, A major
No. 12, B minor

A Second Set of Six Organ Concertos (1740):

No. 1, F major

No. 2, A major

No. 3, G major

No. 4, D major

No. 5, G minor

No. 6, D minor

Hornpipe, D major (1740)

Imeneo (1740)

L'Allegro, il Penseroso ed il Moderato (1740)

March, F major (c. 1740)

Oboe concerto No. 1, B♭ major (1740)

Oboe concerto No. 2, B♭ major (1740)

Song, Love's but the frailty of the mind (1740)

Song, Yes, I'm in love (The 'Je ne sa quoi') (c. 1740)

When Phoebus the tops of the hills does adorn
(A Hunting Song [The Death of the Stag]) (c. 1740)

Deidamia (1741)

Duet, No, di voi non vuo fidarmi (1741)

Duet, Quel fior ch'alla'alba ride (1741)

Duet, Beato in ver che può (1742)

Messiah (1742)

Overture [Suite], D major (c. 1742)

Samson (1743)

Te Deum, 'Dettingen', D major (1743)

The king shall rejoice (Dettingen anthem), D major (1743)

Duet, Fronda leggiera e mobile (c. 1744)

Joseph and his Brethren (1744)

Semele (1744)

Belshazzar (1745)

[Comus] (1745)

Duet, Ahi, nelle sorte umane (1745)

Hercules (1745)

March, G major (c. 1745)

Minuet, D major (1745)

Minuet, D major (1745)

Minuet, G major (c. 1745)

Minuet, G major (c. 1745)

Sinfonia, B♭ major (c. 1745)

Song, Stand round my brave boys (A Song made for
the Gentlemen Volunteers of the City of London) (1745)

Concerto for wind, D major (c. 1746)

Concerto for wind, F major (c. 1746)

March, D major (1746)

March, D major (c. 1746)

Occasional Oratorio (1746)

Organ Concerto, F major (c. 1746)

Song, From scourging rebellion (A Song on the Victory obtained
over the Rebels) (1746)

Concerti a due cori (c. 1747):
No. 1, B♭ major
No. 2, F major
No. 3, F major

Judas Maccabaeus (1747)

March for the Fife, C major (c. 1747)

March for the Fife, D major (c. 1747)

Alexander Balus (1748)

Joshua (1748)

Blessed are they that considereth the poor
(Foundling Hospital Anthem), D minor (1749)

How beautiful are the feet (Anthem on the peace), D minor (1749)

Music for the Royal Fireworks, D major (1749)

Susanna (1749)

Solomon (1749)

Theodora (1750)

The Choice of Hercules (1751)

Jephtha (1752)

Hornpipe, G major (c. 1756)

The Triumph of Time and Truth (1757)

March, F major (1758)

March, C major (1758)

March, C major (1758)

March, D major (1758)

March, D major (1758)

A Third Set of Six Concertos, Opus 7 (publ. 1761):
No. 1, B♭ major
No. 2, A major
No. 3, B♭ major
No. 4, D minor
No. 5, G minor
No. 6, B♭ major

handel

recommended recordings

These recordings are all available at the time of writing (June 1993). I have deliberately listed complete oratorio and opera recordings rather than extracts on the basis that a whole work cannot be understood through familiarity only with fragments. However, extracts from some of the more popular works – notably Messiah – are commonly marketed as 'highlights'. Those who might baulk at the expense of buying, say, three discs instead of one can be strongly reassured that most of Handel's work does not include 'lowlights'. All numbers given are those that apply to the compact disc format. Many recordings can also be bought on conventional tape cassette.

Many works, particularly operas and oratorios, are available in one recording only. While everything listed below is of an extremely high standard of performance and recording, a place in this list does not necessarily indicate quality of a superlative degree. As long as a performance is acceptable, it is better to have the only available recording of a particular work than no recording at all.

Where more than one recording of a work exists and only one is listed, I would emphasize that my choice is based only on personal response and experience. Choosing between two recordings is by no means as clear-cut an exercise as some would have us believe. Therefore my choices are to be taken only as a guide; vehement disagreement is welcomed. My list reveals a strong preference for period-style instruments and techniques. That does not mean, however, that versions on modern instruments are necessarily to be snubbed, even though the current fashion among record companies is to employ specialized baroque orchestras and ensembles for baroque music. Where a recording is known to have been made using modern instruments, it is preceded by a *.

ORCHESTRAL

CONCERTI A DUE CORI
EBS, Gardiner. Philips Dig. 434 154-2.

CONCERTOS FOR OBOE AND STRINGS
Reichenberg, English Concert, Pinnock. DG Dig. 415 291-2.

CONCERTOS FOR ORGAN AND STRINGS (complete)
OP. 4, NOS. 1–6
OP. 7, NOS. 1–6
NOS. 1 IN F, 2 IN A
ARNOLD EDITION: NOS. 1 IN D, 2 IN F
Amsterdam Baroque Orch., Koopman (soloist & dir.).
Erato/Warner Dig. 2292-45394-2 (3).

*OP. 3, 6 CONCERTI GROSSI
ASMF, Marriner. Philips Dig. 426 810-2.

OP. 6, 12 CONCERTI GROSSI
English Concert, Pinnock. DG Dig. 410
897-2, 410 898-2, 410 899-2 (3).

MUSIC FOR THE ROYAL FIREWORKS
CORONATION ANTHEMS
King's Consort, King. Hyp. Dig. CDA 66350 (NB: this recording uses
the original instrumentation, which included twenty-four oboes and
twelve bassoons).

WATER MUSIC
EBS, Gardiner. Philips Dig. 434 122-2.

ORCHESTRAL MUSIC (including Concerti a due cori, Concerti grossi, Music for
the Royal Fireworks, Water Music). English Concert, Pinnock. DG Dig. 423
149-2.

CHAMBER MUSIC
Ecole d'Orphee. CRD 3373/4/5/6/7/8/9/80. (This splendid collection – each disc
available separately – includes all of Handel's Solo and Trio sonatas).

INSTRUMENTAL

Suites for keyboard

No. 1 in A major

No. 2 in F major

No. 3 in D minor

No. 4 in E minor

No. 5 in E major

No. 5a Air and Variations, 'The Harmonious Blacksmith'

No. 6 in F♯ minor

No. 7 in G minor

No. 8 in F minor

Ross. Erato/Warner Dig. 2292-45452-2 (2).

Suites for keyboard, Nos. 1, 2, 4 & 7

Pinnock. DG Dig. 410 656-2.

VOCAL AND CHORAL (INCL ORATORIO)

ACIS AND GALATEA

Burrowes, Rolfe Johnson, Hill, White, King's Consort, King. Hyp.
Dig. CDA 66361/2 (coupled
with Cantata: Look down, harmonious saint).

ALEXANDER'S FEAST

Brown, Watkinson, Stafford, Robson, Varcoe,
Monteverdi Ch., EBS, Gardiner. Philips Dig. 422 055-2.

L'ALLEGRO, IL PENSEROSO ED IL MODERATO

Kwella, McLaughlin, Smith, Ginn, Davies, Hill, Varcoe, Monteverdi Ch.,
EBS, Gardiner. Erato/Warner 2292 45377-2 (2).

ATHALIA

Sutherland, Kirkby, Jones, Bowman, Rolfe Johnson, Thomas,
New College Ch., AAM, Hogwood. O-L Dig. 417 126-2 (2).

BELSHAZZAR

Auger, Robbin, Bowman, Rolfe Johnson, Robertson, Wilson-Johnson,
Wistreich, English Concert, Pinnock. DG 431 793-2 (3).

BROCKES PASSION

Klietmann, Gáti, Zádori, Minter, Statdtsingecher, Capella Savaria, McGegan.
Hung. Dig. HCD12734/6-2.

CANTATAS FOR SOLO VOICE

Kirkby, AAM, Hogwood. O-L Dig. 414 473-2.

CARMELITE VESPERS (including anthem DIXIT DOMINUS)

Feldman, Kirkby, Van Evera, Cable, Nichols, Cornwell, Thomas, Taverner
Ch. & Players, Parrott. EMI Dig. CDS7 49749-2.

CHANDOS ANTHEMS, NOS. 1–11

Dawson, Partridge, The Sixteen Ch. & Orch., Christophers. Chan.
CHAN 8600/0504/0505/0509 (available separately).

*CORONATION ANTHEMS

King's College Ch., Willcocks (1963). Decca Argo 436 256-2
(coupled with Chandos Anthem No. 9: O praise the Lord).

CORONATION ANTHEMS

Westminster Abbey Ch., English Concert, Preston, Pinnock.
DG Dig. 410 030-2.

DETTINGEN TE DEUM; DETTINGEN ANTHEM

Westminster Abbey Ch., English Concert, Preston.

DG Dig. 410 647-2.

ESTHER

Kwella, Rolfe Johnson, Partridge, Thomas, Kirkby, Elliott, Westminster
Cathedral Ch., AAM, Hogwood.

O-L Dig. 414 423-2 (2).

HERCULES

Smith, Walker, Denley, Rolfe Johnson, Tomlinson, Savidge, Monteverdi Ch.,
EBS, Gardiner. DG Dig. 423 137-2 (3).

ISRAEL IN EGYPT

Argenta, Van Evera, Wilson, Rolfe Johnson, Thomas, White, Taverner Ch. &
Players/Parrott. EMI CDS7 54018-2 (2).

JEPHTHA

Robson, Dawson, von Otter, Chance, Varcoe, Holton, Monteverdi Ch., EBS,
Gardiner. Philips Dig. 422 351-2 (3).

JOSHUA

Kirkby, Oliver, Bowman, Ainsley, George, New College Ch., King's
Consort, King. Hyp. Dig. CDA 66461/2.

JUDAS MACCABAEUS

Kirkby, Denley, Bowman, MacDougall, George, King's Consort, King. Hyp.
Dig. CDA 66641/2.

*MESSIAH (HIGHLIGHTS)

McNair, von Otter, Chance, Hadley, Lloyd, ASMF, Marriner.
Philips 434 723-2.

MESSIAH

Nelson, Kirkby, Watkinson, Elliott, Thomas, Christ Church Ch., AAM,
Hogwood. O-L 411 858-2 (3).

MESSIAH

Hunt, Williams, Spence, Minter, Thomas, Parker, Philharmonia Baroque,
McGegan. HM Dig. HMU 907050/52 (3)
(usefully includes many variants as appendix).

*MESSIAH

Price, Schwarz, Burrows, Estes, Bavarian Radio SO, Davis.
Philips Dig. 412 538-2.

MESSIAH

Marshall, Robbin, Rolfe Johnson, Brett, Hale, Shirley-Quirk, Monterverdi
Ch., EBS, Gardiner. Philips 434 297-2 (2).

LA RESURREZIONE DI NOSTRO SIGNOR GESU CRISTO

Saffer, Nelson, Spence, Thomas, George, Philharmonia Baroque, McGegan.
HM Dig. HMU 907027/8.

SAUL

Dawson, Brown, Ragin, Ainsley, Mackie, Salmon, Slane, Miles, Savage,
Monteverdi Ch., EBS, Gardiner. Philips Dig. 426 265-2 (3).

SOLOMON

Watkinson, Argenta, Hendricks, Rodgers, Jones, Rolfe Johnson, Varcoe,
Monteverdi Ch., EBS, Gardiner. Philips Dig. 412 612-2 (2).

SUSANNA

Hunt, Feldman, Minter, J. Thomas, D. Parker, Thomas, Chamber Ch. of
University of California, Philharmonia Baroque, McGegan.
HM Dig. HMC907030/2.

THEODORA

Hunt, Minter, Lane, J. Thomas, D. Thomas, Philharmonia Baroque,
McGegan. HM Dig. HMU 907060/2.

THE TRIUMPH OF TIME AND TRUTH

Poulenard, Smith, Stutzmann, Elwes, Musiciens du Louvre, Minkowski.
Erato/Warner Dig. 2292-45351-2.

THE TRIUMPH OF TIME AND TRUTH

Fisher, Kirkby, Brett, Partridge, Varcoe, London Handel Ch. & Orch.,
Darlow. Hyp. Dig. CDA 66071/2.

UTRECHT TE DEUM AND JUBILATE

Nelson, Kirkby, Brett, Elliott, Covey-Crump, Thomas, Christ Church Ch.,
AAM, Preston. O-L Dig. 414 413-2.

STAGE WORKS (INCLUDING OPERA)

AGRIPPINA

Bradshaw, Saffer, Minter, Hill, Isherwood, Popken, Dean, Banditelli, Sziláagi, Capella Savaria, McGegan. HM Dig. HMU 907063/5.

ALCESTE (INCIDENTAL MUSIC)

Kirkby, Nelson, Kwella, Pound, Cable, Denley, Elliott, Covey-Crump, Thomas, Keyte, AAM, Hogwood. O-L Dig. 421 479-2 (coupled with incidental music for Comus).

ALCINA

Auger, Della Jones, Kuhlmann, Harrhy, Kwella, Tomlinson, Opera Stage Ch., City of London Baroque Sinfonia, Hickox. EMI Dig. CDS7 49771-2 (3).

ALESSANDRO

Jacobs, Boulin, Poulenard, Nirouët, Varcoe, de Mey, La Petite Bande, Kuijken. HM/BMG Dig. GD77110 (3).

AMADIGI DI GAULA

Stutzmann, Smith, Harrhy, Fink, Bertin, Musiciens du Louvre, Minkowski.
Erato/Warner Dig. 2292- 45490-2.

ATALANTA

Farkas, Bartfai-Barta, Lax, Bandi, Gregor, Polgar, Capella Savaria, McGegan.
Hung. Dig. HCD 12612/4.

FLAVIO, RÈ DI LONGOBARDI

Gall, Ragin, Lootens, Fink, Ensemble 415, Jacobs. HM Dig. HMC
901312/3.

FLORIDANTE

Capella Savaria, McGegan. Hung. Dig. HCD 31304/6.

GIULIO CESARE

Larmore, Schlick, Fink, Rorholm, Ragin, Zanasi, Lallouette, Visse, Cologne
Concerto, Jacobs. HM Dig. HMC 901385/7.

MUZIO SCEVOLA, ACT III
Ostendorf, Fortunato, Baird, Mills, Lane, Matthews, Urrey,
Brewer Chamber Orch., Palmer. Newport NPD 85540.

ORLANDO
Bowman, Auger, Robbin, Kirkby, Thomas, AAM, Hogwood. O-L Dig. 430
845-2 (3).

OTTONE
Bowman, McFadden, Smith, Denley, Visse, George, King's Consort, King.
Hyp. Dig. CDA66571/3.

OTTONE
Minter, Saffer, Dean, Gondek, Popken, Spence, Freiburg Baroque Orch.,
McGegan. HM Dig. HMU 907073/5.

IL PASTOR FIDO
Esswood, Farkas, Lukin, Kállay, Flohr, Gregor, Capella Savaria, McGegan.
Hung. Dig. HCD 12912/3 (2).

RODELINDA, REGINA DE LANGOBARDI

Schlick, Schubert, Cordier, Wessel, Prégardieu, Schwarz, Le Stagione, Schneider. HM/BMG Dig. RD 77192 (3).

SIROE, RÈ DI PERSIA

Fortunato, Baird, Ostendorf, Brewer Chamber Orch., Palmer. Newport NCD 60125 (3).

TAMERLANO

Ragin, Robson, Argenta, Chance, Findlay, Schirrer, EBS, Gardiner. Erato/Warner Dig. 2292-45408-2 (3).

TERPSICHORE

Musiciens du Louvre, Minkowski. Erato/Warner Dig. 2292-45806-2.

- ABBREVIATIONS -

AAM *Academy of Ancient Music*
arr. *arranged/arrangement*
ASMF *Academy of St. Martin-in-the-Fields*
attrib. *attributed*
bar. *baritone*
bc. *basso continuo*
bn. *bassoon*
c. *circa*
ch. *chorus/choir/chorale*
Chan. *Chandos*
cl. *clarinet*
CO *Chamber Orchestra*
COE *Chamber Orchestra of Europe*
comp. *composed/composition*
contr. *contralto*
db. *double bass*
DG *Deutsche Grammophon*
Dig. *digital recording*
dir. *director*
ECO *English Chamber Orchestra*
ed. *editor/edited*
edn. *edition*
ens. *ensemble*
fl. *flute*
HM *Harmonia Mundi France*
hn. *horn*
hp. *harp*
hpd. *harpsichord*
Hung. *Hungaroton*

instr. *instrument/instrumental*
kbd. *keyboard*
LSO *London Symphony Orchestra*
Mer. *Meridian*
mez. *mezzo-soprano*
ob. *oboe*
OCO *Orpheus Chamber Orchestra*
orch. *orchestra/orchestral/orchestrated*
org. *organ/organist*
O-L *Oiseau-Lyre*
perc. *percussion*
pf. *pianoforte*
picc. *piccolo*
PO *Philharmonic Orchestra*
qnt. *quintet*
qt. *quartet*
sop. *soprano*
str. *string(s)*
tb. *trombone*
ten. *tenor*
tpt. *trumpet*
trans. *translated/translation*
transcr. *transcribed/transcription*
unacc. *unaccompanied*
va. *viola*
var. *various/variation*
vc. *cello*
vn. *violin*

The following list excludes available modern reprints of eighteenth century sources. Many of the volumes mentioned below include fuller bibliographies. Valuable articles on Handel, with bibliographies, can be found in *The New Grove Dictionary of Music and Musicians*, 20 vols (London, 1980) and on the composer and individual operas in *The New Grove Dictionary of Opera*, 4 vols (London, 1992).

Gerald Abraham ed., *Handel: A Symposium* (London, 1954)

Winton Dean, *Essays on Opera* (Oxford, 1990)

Winton Dean, *Handel and the Opera Seria* (Berkeley and Los Angeles, 1969; London, 1970)

Winton Dean & John Merrill Knapp, *Handel's Operas 1704–1726* (Oxford, 1987)

Edward J Dent, *Handel* (London, 1934)

Otto Deutsch, *Handel, A Documentary Biography* (London, 1955, 1974)

Ellen Harris, *Handel and the Pastoral Tradition* (London, 1980)

Julian Herbage, *Messiah* (London, 1948)

Christopher Hogwood & Richard Luckett eds., *Music in Eighteenth-Century England* (Cambridge, 1983)

Jonathan Keates, *Handel, the Man and his Music* (London, 1985)

Paul Henry Lang, *George Frideric Handel* (New York, 1966, 1977)

Stanley Sadie, *Handel* (London, 1962)

Stanley Sadie, *Handel Concertos* (London, 1972)

Watkins Shaw, *A Textual and Historical Companions to Handel's Messiah* (London, 1965)

Stanley Sadie & Anthony Hicks eds., *Handel Tercentenary Collection* (London, 1987)

Percy Young, *Handel* (London, 1946, 1975)

- Acknowledgements -

The publishers wish to thank the following copyright holders for
their permission to reproduce illustrations supplied:

*Archiv Für Kunst und Geschichte, Berlin; The Bridgeman Art Library;
The Mansell Collection Ltd; E. T. Archive*

1–2. WATER MUSIC   13'26"

    (i) Overture

    (ii) Allegro/Andante/Allegro

    English Chamber Orchestra, Raymond Leppard

    Tradition has it that Handel composed this collection for wind instruments to restore himself to favour with George I. There is no evidence for this but it is possible that it was written for a royal excursion up the River Thames in 1717.

3–7. CONCERTO GROSSO, OP. 6 NO. 1 IN G   10'52"

    I Musici

    Handel's Concerti Grossi (or great concertos) are a superlative example of a form popular in the seventeenth and eighteenth centuries. An early mode of the concerto, they were written for a small group of strings heard both in contrast and in harmony with a larger group.

8. CORONATION ANTHEM, ZADOK THE PRIEST   5'33"

    Academy & Chorus of St Martin in the Fields

    Sir Neville Marriner

    Composed for the coronation of George II at Westminster Abbey in 1727, Zadok the Priest has been sung at every British coronation since. Its ceremonial splendour is heightened by a powerfully charged choral entry.

9. MUSIC FOR THE ROYAL FIREWORKS, OVERTURE   8'24"

English Chamber Orchestra, Raymond Leppard

Written for the open air this piece was played at a fireworks display to mark the Peace of Aix-la-Chapelle, 1749. Handel's original orchestration listed 24 oboes, 12 bassoons, 9 trumpets, 9 hand horns and 4 timpani which create a magnificent wall of sound.

10–12. ORGAN CONCERTO NO. 6   12'07"

Daniel Chorzempa (organ), Concerto Amsterdam, Jaap Schröder

Handel was a virtuoso organist and his organ concertos encapsulate the enthusiasm of the player: melodic, almost catchy, bold and humourous.

13–14. MESSIAH, THEN THE EYES OF THE BLIND SHALL BE OPENED/
HE SHALL FEED HIS FLOCK   5'37"

Helen Watts (mezzo soprano), Heather Harper (soprano)

London Symphony Orchestra, Sir Colin Davis

Charles Jennens prefaced his libretto for the Messiah with the words 'Let us sing of greater things' – the multi-layered meanings, the orchestral plainness, the unbroken inspiration make this oratorio one of the most magestic religious pieces of the Anglican church.

15. MESSIAH, HIS YOKE IS EASY   2'08"
London Symphony Orchestra & Chorus
Sir Colin Davis
*This beautiful, pastoral chorus builds on the musical discoveries of
Handel's earlier Italian duets.*

16. MESSIAH, HALLELUJAH CHORUS   3'51"
London Symphony Orchestra & Chorus
Sir Colin Davis
*A rousing celebratory chorus, this ends the Messiah. At one performance in 1743 the whole
assembly, led by George II, rose to its feet at its opening and remained standing to the end,
such was its power.*

Tracks chosen by Philips Classics; text by Emma Lawson